HALF WAY HOME

HALF WAY HOME

HUGH HOWEY

A John Joseph Adams Book
Mariner Books
Houghton Mifflin Harcourt
Boston   New York
2019

For information about permission to reproduce selections from this book, write to
trade.permissions@hmhco.com or to Permissions, Houghton Mifflin Harcourt
Publishing Company, 3 Park Avenue, 19th Floor, New York, New York 10016.

hmhbooks.com

Library of Congress Cataloging-in-Publication Data
Names: Howey, Hugh, author.
Title: Half way home / Hugh Howey.
Description: Boston ; New York : Houghton Mifflin Harcourt, 2019. | "A John
Joseph Adams Book." | Summary: Nearly sixty teens awaken halfway through
their training, stranded on a harsh alien world with few supplies, no
adults, and led by a treacherous artificial intelligence, but their
greatest enemy is each other.
Identifiers: LCCN 2019009828 (print) | LCCN 2019016641 (ebook) |
ISBN 9780358051817 (ebook) | ISBN 9780358213246 (hardback) |
ISBN 9780358211587 (trade paper)
Subjects: | CYAC: Survival—Fiction. | Space colonies—Fiction. | Artificial
intelligence—Fiction. | Life on other planets—Fiction. | Science
fiction. | BISAC: FICTION / Science Fiction / Adventure.
Classification: LCC PZ7.1.H6886 (ebook) |
LCC PZ7.1.H6886 Hal 2019 (print) |
DDC [Fic]—dc23
LC record available at https://lccn.loc.gov/2019009828

Book design by Carly Miller

Printed in the United States of America

DOC 10 9 8 7 6 5 4 3 2 1

For Carr Murrill

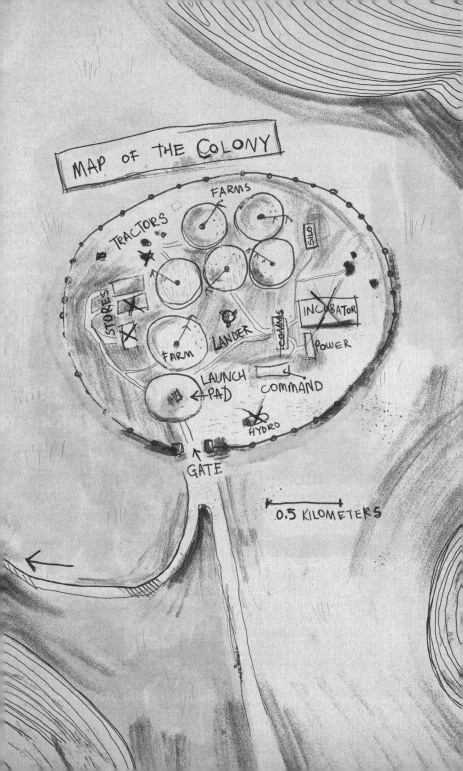

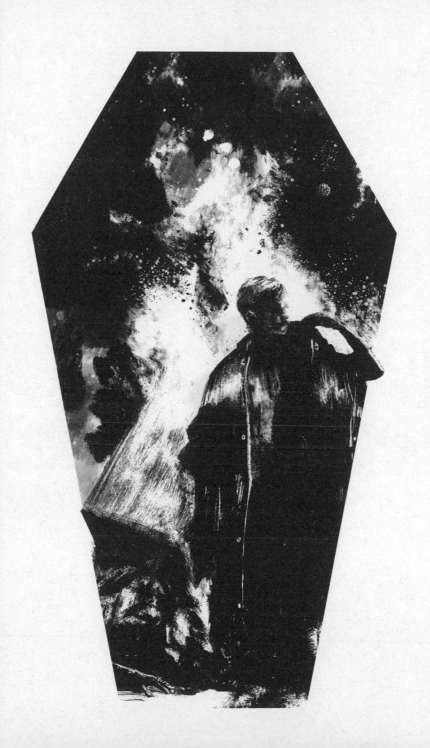

0
WHAT SHOULD HAVE BEEN

I WAS A BLASTOCYST, ONCE. A MERE JUMBLE OF cells clinging to one another. A fertilized egg. Of course, we were all in such a state at some point in our lives, but I excelled at it in a way you didn't. I spent more time in that condition than I have as a person.

Hundreds of years more, in fact.

I still like to imagine myself like that: a shapeless form, quivering and ripe and full of potential. Holding that image in my head makes it seem as if I haven't been born yet, as if we could let things play out one more time and arrive at some different destination. Perhaps it would lead to a new, fuller me.

But repeating the past is as impossible as faster-than-light travel and suspended animation — it's the stuff of the imagination. They're wonderful ideas, but they all lie on the other side of *what-can-be*. So far as we know, anyway.

Hence the quivering eggs of potential, my fellow colonists and me.

What better way to seed the stars with the gift of humanity? Imagine the colony ships, otherwise: They'd be the size of small moons and packed to capacity with living, eating, breathing, defecating humans. Such arks would be impractical, even if those colonists could survive the ensuing insanity of interstellar travel, the hundreds of years of boredom and breeding and infighting that would occur on a slow passage to some distant rock. And what would happen when that rock proved uninhabitable?

Far more sensible, of course, is a system whereby blastocysts such as myself are launched into space with a handful of machines to raise us. Especially considering a colonial failure rate of roughly fifty percent. Every colony lander is nothing more than a flipped coin glimmering in space, the word "viable" printed on one side and "unviable" stamped on the other.

The game — *your* game — is seeing where that coin lands.

At a cost of nine hundred billion each, one might wonder why a nation would take such odds. Then I imagine what it would mean for a mere country to own an entire planet: all those resources, all that precious livable land, a launch pad for further expansion. It would be like an island acquiring a continent. Besides, if you don't do it, someone else will, right? Which means you *must*.

The rewards can be enormous. A single patent on one useful alien gene sequence could fund several more colonies — and so although the process is a huge gamble, it's one that has the potential to be *extremely* lucrative. It becomes just one more way for the wealthiest countries to maintain their wealth. Like a slot machine that dispenses a jackpot with every other coin.

That's what "viable" means: a planet with more reward than risk. A *jackpot*. Not for the aspiring colonists, of course, but certainly for the country that sent them. I bet there are formulae involved, far too complex for one such as myself to understand. With the profession you chose for me, I have a better chance of grasping the vagaries of the human brain. But I can imagine the atmosphere of our new home has to read such-and-such parts per million. Perhaps the mass of the potential planet has to be within certain parameters. And obviously, there can't be hordes of unconquerable predators roaming about.

There are a million variables, I'm sure, but by whatever confluence of events, half the planets pass muster — half of them come up viable, and our reward as little blastocysts is a chemical trigger, a simple compound that causes us to resume our cellular division as if we were in our mother's wombs.

Then, fed through the same amniotic fluid we breathe, we are slowly transformed into pudgy babies, dutiful children, and finally: fully formed adults. All the while, the training programs you wrote teach us the things we need to know. For me, it would be learning to tend to the psychological needs of my fellow colonists—basically keeping the fleshy bits of your engines nicely oiled, putting the gears back together when they break.

The growing process would normally take thirty years. Three decades spent in vats that provide perfect nourishment, our muscles electrically stimulated so they grow strong. And when we emerged, five hundred of us, specialists in each of our own fields, we would begin the arduous task of conquering our new world. We would be the first generation of the hundreds it might take to bring an entire planet to its knees, to extract its resources, to unlock its secrets, and to pay back our startup fee and so much more to some old nation on some old distant rock.

Meanwhile, we'd save up for a further round of expansion. Our thumbs would cock back, a new coin ready to flip out into space.

During those thirty years of gestation, our colony lander would be busy preparing our new home. We would awaken to find it had been growing and dividing alongside us. Tractors that flew a trillion miles would fire up and begin tilling the soil, preparing it for our needs. Mining machines would dig loads of ore from the crust and feed the foundry machines, which would then turn it into alloy so the shaping machines could create, well . . . more machines.

Some of us would probably wonder why we were even needed. But we'd do the jobs we'd been trained for—happy, perhaps, to not know or want anything else. We might one day become positively eager, just as you had, to expand and conquer new worlds, because the real spoils would exceed the value of information transmitted back by satellite. It would dwarf the worth of the sloth-like cargo ships full of minerals and ore.

No, the real allure to this nasty procedure is the immortality. The allegiance of shared genes and imaginary borders that stretch easily across the light-years. The reward of knowing your children are out there, outliving whatever star warmed the planet they were conceived on, your grandchildren outliving *that* new star, and so on.

So much wealth and immortality, all for the flip of a coin.

Of course, that's what *should* have been. There's always the other half of the colonies, the ones that go swiftly and simply. On these, the AI crunches those complex formulae, and something comes up short —who knows why or by how much. Atmospheric toxicity, crushing gravity, imperfect orbits with wild seasonal swings, frequent extinction impactors . . . any of these would spell doom for a settlement colony, and none of these traits could be reliably deduced across hundreds of light-years of space. Your stellar spectrographers with their actuarial tables—they can only make their best guesses and flick their thumbs one way or the other, but it's still a game of chance.

Unviable. That's what the AI would compute. And instead of a molecular trigger setting off my cell division, the machines would deliver a chemical bullet to liquefy me and my fellow colonists. Some engineer actually dubbed this the "Abort Sequence." Five hundred potential humans destroyed with an acid bath, the entire colony set afire and reduced to slag, then the nuclear explosions to make sure not even the ash survives.

One might think that engineer possessed a poor sense of humor— and as one of those blastocysts nearly aborted, I had the same twinge of disgust. Even knowing the etymology of the term, I still recognize it as one of those cruel coincidences that punctuate human existence. Originally coined to describe the termination of an unwanted pregnancy, then co-opted by the aeronautics industry for any terminated trial, the word has found an oddly coincidental return home thanks to the cruelty of planetary colonization.

Why the abort sequence? one could ask. Why reduce so much of your capital investment to lava before setting off thermonuclear detonations? We labored to understand before we learned how dear knowledge had become, that in the war between nations to dominate so much new territory, ideas had transmuted into a new currency recognizable to all and immediately transferable. Intellectual property rights now serve as an ephemeral gold, weightless and invisible, priceless artifacts one can slip into the folds of one's brain and smuggle anywhere, undetected. These tidbits can then be traded by the devious for real wealth or spread by the loose-lipped like a disease.

Data. Our data. Information and patents are now worshipped by all.

Of all the data, perhaps none is so protected as our colony AI, who is as much a clone of our ancestors as we are. Hence the chemical bullet, the fire systems, and the nukes that made the slow journey across eons alongside us—all of them cheap to transport and kind enough to not shit, breathe, and reproduce.

Those are the calculations. *Your* calculations. Viable or abort. The toss of a coin. On or off. One or zero. A dichotomy engineers and scientists adore. The hard edge that gives their intellectual pursuits the ability to slice through data and arrive at *truth*.

As a psychologist, a member of the "soft" sciences, it's the sort of crisp rationality that fills me with envy. Even the quantum physicists have their collapsing wave functions, driving all that fuzziness into numbers as precise and knowable as any other rational field of inquiry.

The problem, however, is that the choice isn't really dichotomous. But you didn't know that, did you? You didn't foresee a third possibility, one as unplanned for as it was unimaginable to you. By leaving the choice of viability or unviability to an artificial intelligence—a consciousness built to model our own thinking—your engineers created a problem that falls under *my* purview as a psychologist.

Something soft.

Two options, viable and unviable, both of them meticulously planned for. Except, if you flip coins often enough, send enough of them into the air, something *else* can happen, something miraculous and yet statistically inevitable. Send out thousands, tens of thousands, hundreds of thousands of colony ships — each another spinning coin — and eventually one of them will surprise you.

One of them will land on its edge and remain there, balanced and wobbling, full of awful or awesome potential. It will be neither heads nor tails but something *else*.

What follows is the account of one of those rare coins.

It is the story of my home.

PART I

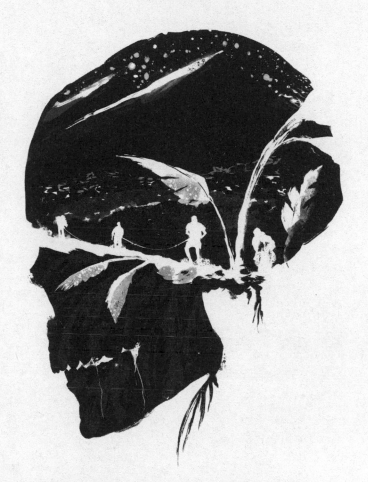

OUT OF THE VAT

1

ABORT

I WAS FIFTEEN YEARS OLD BEFORE I OPENED MY eyes for the first time. Fifteen. Not quite an adult—halfway between boy and man. Before that moment, I had learned everything from visions directly implanted into my brain. I had been stuffed with virtual lessons and life experiences as my body grew inside a vat.

The training programs I grew up with were wont to flit about, out of sequence and irregular. It was often just me and the colony AI in his several guises, maybe a few virtual students to serve as examples or to keep me from going crazy. One minute, I'd be walking through the woods, listening to Colony lecture. The next, I'm in a counseling session, pretending to do therapy with two virtual colonists who can't get along. This jostling of my consciousness feels absolutely normal, for it's all I've ever known.

Then, I woke up. I saw the real world, solid and unyielding, and it made far less sense.

I came to in a square column of glass. The first thing I noticed was a girl waking up in the large vat adjacent to mine. Thick amniotic fluid flowed down our naked bodies, the level receding as the drain at my feet gurgled. Bubbles floated up from the drain and burst on the surface. I vomited two lungfuls of bluish slime, dry heaving, hacking, coughing—my body knowing innately what to do as it began to breathe for the first time. I shivered and wheezed, the air around me cold but able to sear my lungs, burning me and freezing me at once.

I wiped at my stinging eyes; my senses were overwhelmed and confused. I had just been learning regression therapy, and now I found myself in a strange place, naked—but not alone. Lost on me was the ironic reversal of the dreams I had been taught to interpret: the waking up in public with no clothes on.

The girl in the adjoining vat slumped against my glass, her shoulder flattening out where it pressed, her neck straining as she coughed and wiped at her eyes. Both of us were coming into our lives with all the spasms and grace of a torturous death.

My vat slid open on one side and a cacophony of sounds assaulted my unused ears. Just as with my vision, I had been "hearing" for fifteen years, but only by having the auditory centers in my brain directly stimulated. Never had it been through such physical, intimate, sonic violence as this. Noise that presses flesh. Noise like a second heartbeat. Noise you can feel in your bones.

Screams. People shouting. The crackle of . . . flames? Behind it all was an oddly serene voice calling out as if from everywhere: *"Stay calm. Please make your way toward the exit."*

But nothing about the situation was calm. And there was no clear exit.

Were it not for my wobbly legs, I would've thought it an emergency drill. In all my training modules, however, my body had known how to balance itself. That was no longer the case. Even with legs artificially stimulated to remain strong, I struggled to control them.

I grasped the edge of my vat's opening, stepped over the jamb, and joined the narrow stream of other naked and confused colonists beyond. We packed ourselves into the narrow passageway between the empty chambers like animals chuted for slaughter. Slick bodies came into contact with mine, overwhelming more of my senses with bizarre newness.

In the distance, someone yelled, "Fire!" and the already tight space became a horrific crush of human frenzy, of elbows and knees and shoving. Strangers shrieked at the top of their lungs. We became one quivering mass of fear and confusion. Bodies became like cells, forming a new blastocyst with awful potential.

I tried to keep the girl close. We clung to each other like baby chicks, imprinting on and scrambling after the first thing we'd seen upon hatching. Around us, the column of flesh trapped between the vats flowed slowly in one direction. I felt we should be going the *opposite* way, toward the bright light that flickered beyond the scurrying crowd.

Half of us seemed to be working against the rest, everyone canceling out each other in a macabre display of Brownian motion. It wasn't until the thick smoke billowed closer that those of us pushing toward the light recognized it as the danger we were meant to avoid.

Panic vibrated through the crowded mess, sparking from skin to skin as the shrieks of those burning alive reached us ahead of the horrid smell. I lost hold of the girl as someone pushed between us. I watched her face disappear—and then her outstretched hand. The crowd jostled me toward some unseen exit.

My entire trip down the narrow passageway was made in reverse; I looked back for the girl and watched the glow of flames brighten, reflecting off the wet walls of glass to either side. As the mob carried me to safety, some part of my thoughts flitted to the therapy the survivors would need: the grief counseling, the group sessions, to treat the extreme likelihood of severe post-traumatic stress disorder.

I fell backwards through the exit—back into trampled mud and rainy night. I clawed my way, shivering, across a tangle of the filthy and fleeing. And through the panic, I found myself dwelling on my years of training, on what was expected of me, on what I needed to do to fix the situation.

My job is to help people recover from tragedies, I thought.

But where were the people whose job it was to *prevent* them?

*   *   *

The night and rain assaulted us with frigid air, and the flames rising all around us seemed magical in their ability to defy both. Chemical fires, licking mightily through both the chill and wet, seemed all the more powerful for it. More fierce and terrifying.

The last of the survivors stumbled out into the mud—coughing, steaming, tripping over those still scurrying out of the way. They splashed us as they staggered past, arms wide for balance and eyes wide with shock. Beyond them, the screams of those who would never join us reverberated through the vat module. They cried out for help, but we were too busy coming to grips with our own new lives to chance saving theirs.

So few of us seemed to have made it out. Fifty or less—and all of us, of course, mere kids. Naked, covered in mud, we coughed and experimented with breathing. Most struggled to get away from the module, but I crawled back toward it, squeezing through the flow of colonists who fled in the other direction. I searched through them as they went past, looking for the face from my neighboring vat, needing to find something familiar in this new existence.

I found her huddled by the exit, shivering and covered in filth. Our eyes met. Hers were wide and white, little orbs of bewilderment. The film of protective tears on them sparkled as they captured and released the light from the flames.

We collapsed together without speaking and held one another, our chins resting on each other's shoulders, our bodies quivering from the cold and fear.

"The command module!" someone yelled.

I heard feet slap against the mud as fellow colonists ran off to save the dying thing that had birthed us. The girl pulled away from me and watched them go, then turned and followed my gaze down the aisle of vats and to the growing inferno beyond. The screams within the flames had morphed into moans of agony. Hundreds were dying or were already dead.

"We can't save them," she croaked, her voice raspy from coughing and disuse. I turned to her, watched her delicate neck constrict as she swallowed forcefully. A lump under the splatter of mud rose up her neck as if for some purpose, then fell back down. "We have to save Colony," she whispered.

I nodded, but my attention was pulled back to the flames. A dark form moved across the fire, arms waving, the silhouette of dripping flesh visible like a thing sloughing off its shadow. One of the glass walls exploded from the heat, and smoke quickly swallowed the form. Only the moans remained as a newborn near adulthood made the mere handful of sounds it would ever be allowed to.

The girl rose. I turned to her and away from the dying. Large drops of rain spotted the mud on her chest with dollops of pink exposed flesh. She pulled me up and tugged me, staggering, away from the vats. We held each other clumsily, four legs proving more stable than two, as we joined the others in running.

Running and surviving.

2

COMMAND MODULE

WE WERE TOO LATE TO HELP THE COMMAND MOD-
ule. By the time we splashed through the rain to assist the small structure, we found it had already helped itself. Large construction tractors
stood poised over it, their buckets dripping the muddy remnants of
its salvation. Through a small single door, plumes of fire-extinguish-
ing agent billowed out into the wet night. Both efforts to fight the fire
created the illusion that the module was one of us: slathered in mud,
its labored breath visible, all the same marks of desperate self-preservation.

A fellow male colonist came to a stop beside me. He bent over and
rested his hands on his knees and shook his head. His skin was darker
than mine, and he must've been a head taller than me.

"What about us?" he asked.

The boy's body bulged with large muscles. Something in my early
training came back, how we were all made different so the colony
would be stronger. But looking at him, I wondered why the colony
didn't make us all look this way. I felt pale and small beside him.

I rested a hand on his back and bent down beside him. He wasn't
breathing hard, just leaning on his knees as if weighed down by the
gravity of our situation.

I watched a few colonists run past us to gather by the command module and wait for the smoke to clear. The girl — my birth neighbor — fell to her knees beside me and stared at her palms.

"Are you hurt?" I asked. My voice sounded raspy and foreign to my own ears as I used it for the first time outside my dreams.

The girl shook her head. Her hair, groomed by the vat for many years, was now matted in muddy clumps and dripping with rain.

"What happened?" she asked.

"Lightning," the boy beside me whispered. He turned his head sideways and glanced up through the rain, almost as if waiting to be struck down for the accusation. I watched a rivulet of water course down his neck, plowing a track through the mud. He turned to me and slapped his chest. "I'm Kelvin," he said. "A farmer."

I took it as a flash of credentials for his weather theory, rather than an introduction.

"Tarsi," the girl beside me whispered. She continued to stare into her cupped palms as she said it. The brown water gathered there splashed with the trickles from her face. "Teacher," she added, after a pause.

"What about you?" Kelvin asked.

Several more colonists ran by, looking for something to do or somewhere to go. The screams and shouts had turned to panting punctuated with occasional raspy coughs.

"My name's Porter," I told him. I stood, shaking the mud off my hands before helping the girl stand.

"This wasn't lightning," she said.

She turned to us, her face growing dim as the flames from the command module were brought under control. "This was an abort sequence." She waved an arm at the destruction on all sides, at the dozen metal buildings on fire and illuminating the darkness beyond. "Too many modules are on fire for this to be anything else." Tarsi faced us. "The colony AI did this," she said.

"And then changed its mind?" Kelvin shook his head. "Why wake us up?"

"We need to find out," Tarsi said.

She set off toward the command module. I watched her bare feet throw up twin sprays of mud, her naked form blending in with all the people running through puddles, hacking and breathing hard.

Kelvin and I glanced at each other; the streaks of grime on his face did little to conceal the worry in his furrowed brow. He coughed once into a fist, slapped me on the shoulder, then ran through the rain after Tarsi.

I followed him. I was too confused to do otherwise, and too terrified to be alone.

When Kelvin and I reached the command module, we found Tarsi conferring with a couple by the door. Boy and girl, they were huddled together under the slight overhang of the entrance, their backs to the dark, mud-splashed steel.

"What's going on?" I heard Tarsi ask them.

The boy shook his head and jabbed a thumb at the door. Artificial light spilled out of the module, giving me a good look at the couple. I noticed Tarsi and the other girl covering themselves with their arms and was reminded of my own nakedness. My professional curiosity was piqued. Had a training program taught us to be ashamed? I couldn't remember.

Flushed with guilt for even concerning myself with such matters, I shook my head and tried to focus on the crisis around us. Tarsi patted the girl on the arm and stepped into the light; Kelvin followed. Both seemed to be holding it together better than I was, making me long to have been born a teacher or a farmer.

Entering the module, the patter of rain on mud was drowned out by the roar of it against the metal roof. Over that, I could hear the AI speaking, his voice filling the enclosed space:

"—the primary goal. Once the launch pad has been restored, a mission-critical package will be prepared. All efforts must be prioritized for this task."

The voice felt like a warm fluid rising, wrapping around and filling every crevice of my being. For so many years, its constant and soothing sound had been my only company as it emanated from dozens of instructional avatars. For fifteen years, it had readied me for life—teaching and preparing me.

But not for this.

Nearly a dozen colonists had packed themselves into the command module; most sat on the floor with their arms wrapped around their knees. White fire retardant covered every surface like a thin layer of frost. Overhead, a swirling black mist of smoke hovered near the ceiling. There seemed to be minimal fire damage. If the AI was responsible, it would've initiated its own destruction last in order to oversee the process. What I was seeing lent considerable weight to Tarsi's theory.

I followed her and Kelvin as the two of them squeezed down a tight corridor lined with electrical cabinets and headed toward the front of the module. Wracking my memory, I tried to recall where the power for this module came from but couldn't. Another pang of fear roiled up through me as I wondered how many important things I was supposed to know—but hadn't yet learned. We'd been given no orientation for our planet. Nothing at all. We should've had another fifteen years in the vats to learn and grow.

The module widened toward the end, opening on a handful of naked, muddy colonists crowded around a bank of monitors. Three colonists sat in chairs bolted down in front of the screens. All the blinking lights and complex machines made us look even more like lost savages—out of any element we could have possibly been designed for.

Kelvin and Tarsi slid down against one of the walls, and I joined them. Across from us, a few other colonists hugged their knees for warmth or modesty—perhaps both. The three of us followed suit, wrapping our arms around our shins. I could hear several sets of teeth chattering, creating a frantic backbeat for the peppering rainfall and the oddly calm conversation taking place around us.

"Understood, Colony," said a young man sitting in the center chair of the control console. "But as I said, there are some more . . . *primary* needs to tend to. Where are our clothes? Our food? We are— I have a lot of colonists in shock right now. Modules are still burning, and what you're asking will take time."

I admired the young man's poise. He seemed distraught yet in control. He rested his elbows on the counter in front of him, his fingers interlocked above his head as he bent over in worry or deep thought. But it was his voice—the tenor and pace of it matching the AI for calmness—that soothed me. It was as if they were on solid footing. Like together, they could make everything okay.

"I have already recalled two more tractors from mining station two," Colony said. *"It will be two days before they arrive with more supplies. Until then, there are tarps you can repurpose for clothing. The server module, the power modules, and this module will provide adequate shelter. The planet has some caloric resources, enough to last you the duration of the task. I am setting a two-week timetable for the launch of the mission package."*

A girl seated at the console stiffened. "Two weeks?" she asked, turning to the boy who had taken the lead. He held up his hand and nodded to her, then looked around at the rest of us. His eyes widened, as if surprised at how quickly his audience had grown. I leaned away from the wall and looked back down the aisle. Another dozen or so colonists had squeezed into the module to get out of the rain, or perhaps to take stock of themselves, their fellow survivors, and the situation.

"Two weeks seems a bit quick to get something into orbit," the boy said, looking at us rather than facing the monitor. He seemed to be sizing up the group. Taking our measure. "It'll take a few days just to clean up, organize supplies, and—"

"All of that will have to wait. The mission package comes first. The viability of this colony is still in question."

"In *question?*" someone asked. "Fifteen years, and our viability is in *question?*"

The boy in the chair raised his hand, palm out, but nodded to the speaker. With his brow furrowed and his lips pursed, he wore a mask of complete empathy. I immediately fell for the guy, suddenly found myself willing and eager to follow him anywhere, completely trusting in his leadership. Or maybe I was still just being a scared little boy, or a young hatchling looking for something or someone to keep me safe.

He turned to the console and lowered his voice, which brought the whispering in the back of the module to a halt as those gathered there strained to hear. "Colony, what happened? I've got—I don't know— sixty survivors out here? None of us are more than halfway through our training programs. Modules are burning—"

"Ask Colony if he tried to abort us," one of the seated kids said.

The boy waved again, more impatiently this time. "Modules are burning to the ground, and you're asking me to ready a rocket? We need more information. We need help sorting out the base—"

"Sorting out *ourselves*," someone in the back said.

The boy in the seat sighed, shaking his head. "What do you mean about our viability? What is—?"

"Enough!"

Our heads spun as one and peered down the module toward the source of the outburst. A large male—bigger than Kelvin—pushed his way through the crease of shivering teens. He had short, dark hair and even darker eyes. Around his waist he'd tied some electrical wiring. A square of canvas hung from it, covering his groin.

"Out of the chair," he told the speaker, jerking his thumb.

The seated boy rose but did not step away. He stood, fully naked, exuding confidence. I should have risen as well, urging calm between the two boys, but I was just as paralyzed as the others. All of us watched the scene unfold like spectators in glass cages.

"I'm Stevens," the smaller boy said, holding out his hand. "Mechanical foreman, third group. I'm colonist four-four-two—"

"Don't pull rank with me," the bigger kid said. He moved forward, standing right in front of the three of us. Caked mud fell off his enormous thighs and landed near my feet. I reached over and groped for Tarsi's hand, interlocking it with my own. I noticed Kelvin had done the same with her other one.

"I'm Hickson," the large colonist said. He did so quite loudly, as if he meant to address us all. "Third-shift mine security," he continued. "Until a higher-ranking officer comes forward, I'm in charge."

"*Colony* is in charge," Tarsi said.

Her voice, so close by and assertive, startled me. I felt a tinge of anger for drawing attention to ourselves, then shame for feeling *that*.

Hickson swung a large hand down and pointed a finger at each of us, as if we'd all spoken up. "That's right," he said. "Colony is in charge. And my job is to make sure we stay on point." He turned and aimed his finger at Stevens. "It sounds to me like you want to question everything—"

"That's enough," Colony said, and everyone fell silent. *"Hickson, as four-four-seven, you are outranked, but I do appreciate your enthusiasm. Each of you will play vital roles in the weeks ahead. As unusual as the circumstances are, no colony is settled without its unique challenges. I assure you all, your services will be most appreciated, and this colony will be highly touted in future training modules. I'm sure of it.*

"Now, you are all cold and confused, I understand that. The power station, the relay module, and the command module are all under control. I'm bringing the remaining construction vehicles back to camp. There should be plenty of room for everyone to rest and dry out. Tomorrow, work begins. All for the glory of the colony."

"For the glory of the colony," everyone echoed back, myself included.

And there was no question whether *that* response had been innate or learned.

No question at all.

3

MOURNING

THAT FIRST NIGHT, I HAD AWFUL AND YET COM-
forting dreams. They were awful in their content, but comforting in
their delivery. They came out of sequence. Random. And the sense
of familiarity brought relief, like I had crawled back into my simulated youth. But what I saw in those fragmented visions tormented
me: colonists burning alive; kids drowning in air, unable to breathe;
me, pounding my fists on a glass column filled with warm, life-giving
fluids, but unable to get inside.

I startled awake, returning to the real and jarred by its consistency.
It made my first morning feel nearly as surreal as my birth the day before.

I rubbed my eyes and sat up. Four of us had ended up sleeping in
the transport cab of a farming tractor. A kid named Oliver and I had
volunteered to sleep on the floor while Kelvin and Tarsi stretched out
on the single bench seat behind us. I stood up quietly and reached for
the scrap of canvas I'd been given the night before. Draping it over my
shoulders, I opened the door to the cab and stepped out into the dim
light of dawn.

Standing on the grated metal of the mining tractor's deck hurt my
bare feet, so I moved out to the smooth hood in front, which was nothing more than a large metal box to shield the vehicle's motor. The sur-

face was still wet with rain, and the thin metal popped as it dented beneath my weight. From my new vantage spot—a good fifteen feet off the ground—I could survey most of the colony base.

It was a depressing sight.

Smoldering modules dotted a wide clearing. Wisps of smoke continued to rise from several of the structures, their original outlines barely visible. I traced our trampled path from the tractor back to the command module, and from there to the vat module, and gasped at the sight. The roof of the enormous unit had caved in on one side, melting inward. We had a rough estimate of the number of survivors, and subtracting that pitiful number from the original five hundred colonists equaled an unfathomable loss of life.

The night before, listening to the AI tell us what needed to be done, I had imagined his soothing voice would be what led us out of trouble. Seeing what was left of base—suspecting that Tarsi had been right about the abort attempt—I staggered under the blow of an even worse realization: The AI had nearly committed genocide. It had nearly wiped us all out due to some unknown calculation.

Tilting my head back, I gazed up at the sky. I'd seen it plenty in my training modules, but what loomed above was different. A tangle of foliage formed a near-solid canopy over our expansive clearing. Remnants of last night's rain leaked through, but hardly any direct sunlight made it to the forest floor. To all sides of our base, far in the distance, enormous trees rose up like cliff faces, their girth wider than the entire colony complex. I had to remind myself that they weren't *actually* trees, but rather some sort of alien analogue.

The tractor door clicked open behind me. I turned around to find Oliver stepping from the cab landing and up to the hood. He was even smaller than me and thin, and the dented metal I was standing on didn't make a sound as it absorbed his weight. Wrapped up in a scrap of canvas, he looked like a piece of insulated wire. His scrawny neck was topped with a roundish head full of coppery auburn hair augmented by streaks of red mud.

"Blessed morning," he said, nodding at me and smiling.

"I hope I didn't wake you," I said, a little taken aback to find him just as chipper as he'd been the night before.

He shook his head and moved to the end of the hood. He dangled his toes over the edge, lifting his face and closing his eyes. I watched his smile broaden; his shoulders rose up as he sucked in a deep breath of air.

The previous night, we'd found Oliver standing in the rain, his arms outstretched, his palms flat. He had been shivering — almost on the verge of hypothermia — but as happy as could be. Tarsi thought he was in shock; Kelvin had stepped on my occupational toes by diagnosing him as "horseshit crazy." The truth had been far more inglorious than either, but more troubling.

Oliver was the colony philosopher, one of the lowliest jobs within our hierarchy. In some ways, I found him to be a kindred spirit. Our occupations were both in the soft sciences and meant to help the other fields cross from the shores of one theory to another, fording the uncertainty between. With his position near the end of the vat (and subsequently one of the lowest ranked among us), Oliver's profession must've been one of those tacked on in an attempt to fill an arbitrary round number. Five hundred colonists had been decided upon, even if not all of us were needed.

Oliver scanned the half-ruined base, his smile never faltering. He then sank down to a seated position, legs crossed. His unusual behavior highlighted a severe problem facing our colony, one that I would need to be aware of in myself. Our training had been interrupted. Cut short. It would be little different than Tarsi teaching the next generation for nine years before kicking them out of her classroom. My own studies had been terminated between the shift from behavioral psychology to evolutionary psychology, sometime in the late twentieth century. What miracles of mental health had I missed in my learning? Was there something more I could've done last night? Something I should be doing right then? Not knowing filled me with dread, as if I were missing a limb I never knew I had and therefore unable to appreciate its absence.

"The gods are surely blessing us with the weather," Oliver said, looking back at me.

I forced myself to return his smile, but I felt sorry for his perpetual bliss. Oliver had only completed half his philosophy training; he seemed to be stuck in older, mostly religious considerations. He had talked us to sleep the night before, going on and on about the wonders of all the gods' creations. He had seen it as a miracle that rain fell upon us as we needed our fires quenched.

Kelvin had tried to explain the atmospheric phenomenon of rain from his farming lessons, and how chemical fires were actually made worse by water, but he failed to demystify the experience for Oliver.

Tarsi, meanwhile, had inquired which gods had started the fires — or failed to prevent them. I was pretty sure her comments didn't come from any of her teaching lessons and, anyway, they posed no threat to Oliver's exuberance.

"Morning," someone said behind me.

I turned and saw Tarsi standing on the landing, her face still streaked with mud. A scrap of canvas draped over her shoulder was cinched around her waist with electrical cable. I stepped back and offered my hand, helping her onto the tractor's hood, which had become something of a porch with no railing. She shivered momentarily as she surveyed our surroundings. I looked out as well and noticed the first few colonists moving from the intact modules. We all seemed to be rising at the same hour — a trait, perhaps, born out of the shared pulsings from within our adjoining wombs.

"How are you holding up?" I asked her. I freed one of my arms from the tarp and wrapped it around her shoulders.

She shook her head. "I had crazy dreams. Waking up this morning wasn't . . . I had hoped last night was some bizarre training module."

I squeezed her shoulder through her makeshift clothing, empathizing completely. "I can feel the difference now," I said. "The difference between being awake and whatever we were before."

"How did this happen?" she whispered.

"I don't know," I admitted.

"The gods work in mysterious ways," Oliver said, smiling up at us.

We all met—as we had agreed to the night before—just outside the command module. The mud-caked and morose shuffled in from all directions like refugees displaced by war. The shredded-tarp fashion seemed near-universal, but many of the colonists had cut slits in theirs, popping their heads through them and thereby freeing their arms. A few colonists wore zipped-up hazard suits they had pulled from intact emergency kits. They looked like aliens among us, shiny and new.

Seeing the looks these colonists got from the others—and recognizing the early signs of in-grouping and out-grouping—I wasn't at all envious of their garb. Nor did I expect the look to last, despite the obvious advantages. The social discomfort in those things had to be worse than the physical annoyances provided by the rough canvas fabric.

The four of us in our sleeping group merged with another small group from a neighboring tractor. Together, we melded with the audience that had formed around the command unit's door. Stevens—the boy who had conversed with Colony the night before—stood just outside the module and spoke with a few other colonists. I scanned the crowd and saw several faces I recognized, including Hickson, the big mine security guy. I noticed the way he kept shifting from one foot to the other as he chewed on his lower lip.

"Listen up, everyone," Stevens said, raising his hands. "If you'll please hold still, Myra is going to get a head count. As stragglers arrive, let's have them come to this side so we don't miss them."

The girl sitting in one of the computer chairs the night before came forward and jabbed the air with her finger. Her lips moved with a count of the not-dead. Stevens ran his hands through his hair, then clasped them behind his back. He looked out at us with a grim expression, his lips pressed thin.

"These are unusual circumstances," he said, "and they are going to call for an unusual force of will, and of cooperation. Colony has awakened us fifteen years early after briefly deciding our settlement was unviable—"

A murmur coursed through the crowd, swelling to a grumbling. Stevens held his hands out, his elbows at his waist. "I understand," he said. "Nobody was closer to the fire than me." He shook his head. Even from a dozen paces away, I could see his cheeks quivering. I felt a sudden urge to run to him, but he was able to win back his stoic mask.

"If you've had your orientation training module, you know how this works. Colony has been teetering between viable and abort since year one. Our new home has much to offer us, but it has many risks as well. I can promise you this, we *will* make it work."

"That's not what Colony said," Hickson blurted out. He turned toward the gathered masses. "Colony definitely said 'unviable' last night. I heard it."

The grumblings returned, several of the colonists shifting about uncomfortably. I became distracted by Myra, who cursed at the movement and started jabbing her finger at our side of the crowd once again.

"People, listen to me," Stevens said. "Hickson has half the story, and I know it's easier to believe the worst, but we must stay strong through this. We are awake for a reason—"

"The mission package," Hickson told the crowd. "We have a very important task, a directive from Colony itself."

Stevens clapped his hands together loudly, but the colonists had begun talking among themselves, creating a dull roar of impossible-to-follow discussions. I felt Kelvin brush up against me and watched him step out between those assembled and the command module.

"Listen up!" he yelled, his voice booming above the din. He had his tarp wrapped around his waist, his wide chest exposed and smeared with dirt. I found myself oddly fascinated by the large sweep of his neck down to his broad, rounded shoulders. His stomach rippled, bunched with knots of muscle as he yelled the crowd to attention. The force of it all stirred something inside me, something that likely merited my professional attention.

Tarsi moved close in his absence as the crowd stilled. I wrapped my arm around her, feeling as protective over her as a mother hen might. Kelvin nodded to Stevens and walked back over to join us, frowning at me as if disappointed by the behavior of the rest of the colonists, his eyes darting between Tarsi and myself.

"Raise your hand if you want to die in the next few days," Stevens said. He stepped away from the command module and scanned our faces. "If any of you want to die, if you feel a mad compulsion to not live among us, please take your bickering and move on. I have not slept a wink, staying up all night to converse with Colony as I made a case for our long-term survival. If any of you want to live on half-truths and innuendo, please go elsewhere." He locked eyes with Hickson as he said this.

"We *do* have an important mission, but we will also devote time to settling this world. The local star"—he pointed up, even though its rays barely filtered through the canopy overhead—"was once given a name by Terran astronomers. We will rename it. We will rename this planet, but *not* before we scratch a toehold in it. If you trust in me, I promise you we will overcome our challenges. Colony was halfway through the construction phase, which means no protein generators and no farms cleared."

He held up one hand and ticked off three fingers with the other. "Food, shelter, and clothing," he said. "Those are our survival priorities. We have enough water collected from the rains to filter and last us for at least a week or two. The rains here are supposedly frequent, so we will not want for bathing and drinking water."

Stevens nodded to Myra, who had rejoined the small leadership group by the module's door. "What did you come to?"

"Fifty-nine," she whispered, but we all heard the count.

A moan slid through the crowd; I could feel myself contributing to it. Not that I had expected much more, but the harsh finality of the number squeezed the air out of my chest. It couldn't be sixty, or sixty-five. Our hopes had been given mathematical limits. The fuzziness of wishes had collapsed into solid dread.

"I want all the sciences to this side," Stevens said, pointing to our half of the crowd. I looked at Tarsi and Kelvin, wondering who among us qualified. I think the entire gathering became confused. We shuffled in place as we discussed our professions with strangers and debated with each other.

"That includes anyone with mechanical or electrical aptitude. All the construction personnel, including miners and farmers, please come forward. Anyone with support occupations, please go over that way."

"I guess I'm over there," Kelvin said, raising his arms and frowning.

Tarsi squeezed his arm and nodded. "I'm going to go over to the support side. I have a feeling we'll be the ones cleaning up this mess."

"I'm staying here," I said. "I guess we'll meet back up tonight?" They nodded, and I gave each of them a quick hug.

Oliver slid up beside me as the other two departed. We were soon joined by almost a dozen other colonists; we took turns introducing ourselves and our professions. Some—like Mica, a geologist—knew they belonged among the scientists. Others, such as an electrician named Karl, weren't sure if they should be with us or with the construction crew.

Several colonists were clearly fudging the semantics of their occupational labels in order to remain together. I watched Tarsi introduce herself to some people in her group and began to think of myself more as a health worker, clearly a sector of support. But before I could pull myself away, Stevens approached our group and began to address us.

"I heard we have an electrical engineer over here?"

Karl raised his hand. "More of an electrician, sir. My name's Karl."

"Where were you in your training?" Stevens asked.

"In the middle of integrated circuit troubleshooting. I don't have any design training, except in basic wiring."

"That's fine," Stevens said. He scanned the group. "Do we have any chemists or chemical engineers?"

"What're we building?" I asked Stevens. "It might be better to know that, and then see what any of us have to offer."

He smiled at me, which made chill bumps explode across my skin, my entire body shivering. I rubbed my hands up and down my arms to fake being cold, feeling anything *but*.

"Good thinking," Stevens said. "What's your name?"

"Porter," I said, reaching out my hand. "Psychologist."

He grasped it firmly and shook it. "That's a science?" he asked, his eyes narrowing.

"Human behavioral science, sir. I'm an engineer of people."

It felt ridiculous as soon as I said it.

"Hmm. I'd like to speak to you privately in a minute." He turned to the others. "Porter's right. Let me tell you what we're going to build, and you let me know how you can help. Be creative. If you can offer support in any area, please let me know."

He paused. "We're building a rocket. Well, the construction guys are building the rocket—what I need from you is the *payload*. Colony is generating most of the schematics, so this will primarily be a building challenge, not a design one. I need people who can solder, who can troubleshoot kinks, and who can double-check every joint and connection during fabrication."

"Why a rocket?" someone asked. "What's the payload?"

"Information," Stevens said. He immediately raised his hands. "No, I don't know what the information is, and we will probably never be told. Whatever it is, Colony won't even trust the communication satellites to transmit it back to Earth. It has to be a hardcopy, so you know how sensitive it must be."

"You've got to be kidding," one of our group said.

"I'm dead serious. Colony is, anyway. Whatever it is, it has the AI riled up. I'm lucky I convinced it to divide us up three ways, so one group can work on helping us survive long-term. All the AI cares about is getting this data off the ground and heading back to Earth, which means *we* need to make that our top priority, or we get no help from Colony in making this our home. Everyone understand?"

We all nodded, looking at one another to search for signs of dissent.

"Karl, I want you to check with the group by the command module to see about those wiring schematics. The rest of you: Today is about scavenging for supplies and setting up our workspaces. I want you to use the power module for your work, but make it so people still have room to sleep. The supply group will tend to your clothing and food, so ignore those grumbling stomachs for a few hours and concentrate on the task at hand. If any of you have chemical training, I want you to liaison with the construction crew—acquiring propellant is going to be a major task. Colony has the mining tractors at our disposal, but we're going to need a place for refinement, probably the fuel depot." Stevens smiled at us. "Okay, good luck today. I'll check in with you before dinner."

He pulled me aside, nodding to the others as they started disbursing. "So, what's your prognosis?" he asked. "For the colonists, I mean."

We stepped away from the scientists and stood in the small clearing that had formed between the three groups. I watched Tarsi speak with two other colonists, her head nodding. I wondered if by the end of the day, she would feel more connected with them than she felt with me.

"I'm not sure," I said. I shook my head and tried to concentrate on the question. I looked Stevens in the eyes. "I'm not even sure how *I'm* doing, to be honest. I think you're doing a great job of keeping things organized, of giving us a sense of purpose. That's really important right now."

"Yeah," Stevens said, looking tired all of a sudden. He flapped back his poncho and pulled a knife out of a scabbard tied around his waist.

He motioned for my tarp, and I relinquished it, trying to act comfortable with my nakedness.

"I figure people need to stay busy to keep their minds from wandering." He inserted the blade in the middle of the canvas and made a quick gash. "Honestly, though, I wish the abort sequence went in the opposite order as the birth sequence."

I nodded, having had the same morbid thought. The lowest-ranked colonists were wakened last, but that also meant we were the last to be aborted. That left the least qualified in charge of our half-wrecked colony.

Stevens held out the poncho he'd just made, and I bowed slightly, letting him drape it over my head.

"I don't think they ever planned on an abort sequence being terminated," I said.

"Aborting the abortion?"

I smiled, more out of duty than any real sense of mirth. "Did Colony say what happened?" I asked.

Stevens shook his head, but I saw something flash across his face. Something he was holding inside, a little twitch I had been trained to recognize.

"No, but it must've happened fast. Colony changed its mind midstream."

I looked toward the command module. "Does it think like us? I didn't think we'd mastered the human brain like that."

"I don't know that we have," Stevens said. "Maybe it made a discovery after the sequence had already begun, or a difficult calculation finally spat out some conflicting result. We may never know."

He patted me on the shoulder. "I want you to keep me abreast of any problems you see. If you get any ideas on what to do about Hickson, I'd love to hear them."

"You should find something for him to kill," I said.

Stevens's eyes widened. "Do what?"

"Some predators. Anything that threatens the group. The guy is programmed for security, and right now *you're* the threat. You need to find something outside our group to unleash him on."

Stevens nodded, his brow furrowing in thought.

"You're right. Absolutely right. But I really hope we don't find anything like that out there. Colony is being pretty mum on what we can expect. Very secretive. I tried all night to pry something out of it." He shook his head, was clearly exhausted.

I clasped Stevens's shoulder as he looked around at the other groups. "We'll figure it out," I told him. "On our own."

"Yeah," he said. He nodded, but the corners of his mouth went down instead of up. Another of those little signs I'd been schooled to note.

"All for the glory of the colony," he muttered.

I nodded but felt no compulsion to answer.

4

SALVAGE

A FEW HOURS AFTER MY TALK WITH STEVENS, I found myself back in the place of my birth: the charred remains of the vat module. I was working there, pulling wire from the conduits below the decking, when he died. At first, I had no idea anything had happened. The base had been a blur of activity all morning—people shouting over the roar of the tractors, excited scavengers running to and fro with special finds.

When the accident occurred, it must have been more of the same noise, blending in with the rest.

Terri, another of the quasi-scientists, was working down the line of vats with me. She pulled up panels of deck plating while I followed behind, cutting open conduits and removing the intact wire. We rolled it up into coils before one of the others took it outside and arranged the scraps.

Beyond us—farther down the aisle of vats—members of the support crew performed the nasty job of dealing with the remains of the dead, which consisted mostly of bone, ash, and sludge. They swept and shoveled the piles onto tarps, then carried them by the corners out through several new holes that had been cut in the sides of the module.

Those holes let in a little light and the barest movement of fresh air. They also let both groups work simultaneously, giving us multiple exit points for taking out items useful or dead.

We found out about Stevens from Tarsi. I heard her yelling my name outside the module, and I half expected her to come in with some sort of lunch. Instead, she ran down the loose decking we'd already picked through, her poncho flapping, her face red and chapped. She was out of breath when she reached me; she grabbed my arm and pulled me toward the exit.

"What's going on?" I asked.

"Stevens," she gasped. "He — he's dead."

I shook my head and tried to pull my arm free, my body revolting. "No," I said. "I was just with him, not three or four hours ago." I looked to Terri, hoping she would back me up, but she remained by the last grate she'd opened, her face slack, her eyes out of focus.

Tarsi pulled me past our old adjoining vats and through the door. I stumbled along, my brain reeling with the idea that someone I had just come to know might be gone forever.

I ran alongside Tarsi and noticed many others hurrying in the same direction. Several groups of colonists were walking the opposite way, their hands over their mouths or tangled up in their hair. We, the running, had a shared look of doubting shock on our faces. The others — the walking — had a similar horrified expression, but with all the disbelief removed.

I followed Tarsi around a large brown puddle of yesterday's rain and across the packed earth. We crested a rise and came to a broad clearing, the spot they'd chosen for the launch pad. Several tractors and dozers idled there, puffing smoke into the sky like gasps of anxious energy. Near one of the tractors, a small cluster of colonists stood around a tarp covering . . . something.

I shuffled down the slope and stopped one of the female colonists who was wandering back up. "What happened?" I asked.

"One of the tractors lurched," she said. "He fell off and got caught under the treads—"

Tarsi dragged me away from the girl and toward the scene.

"We're supposed to get back to work—" the girl called after us.

I stopped at the edge of a small group that had formed near the tarp. Myra sat on the other side of the covered hump, sobbing into her hands, her shoulders shaking. I could see a hand sticking out from under the canvas, half-opened. The fingers curling up from the ground were perfectly still.

"How?" I asked. It didn't make sense. Someone so alive, so in control, was no more. He would never again move of his own volition. Never speak to us with his calm voice. Never lead us to all the hopeful futures he seemed intent on taking us to. I found myself passing through the denial stage and was completely aware of it.

"It wasn't an accident," someone in the group said.

Several other people arrived at a run, while others shuffled off in a state of shock. I was dead-still, undergoing the transformation.

"It was a fluke," another person said. "He fell. I saw it happen."

"Hickson was on the tractor with him," the first boy said. "No way was this an accident."

I turned to tell the two guys to leave it alone, then saw Oliver. Our eyes met, and he came over to me; he wrapped both hands around my elbow, the weight of his thin arms pulling down on mine.

"The gods hath more need of him than we," he said, the barest of smiles on his lips.

"Not now," I told Oliver. I approached the two arguing colonists. They were both males—large, like members of the working class. "Which of you saw what happened?" I asked.

"We both did, I guess."

"I was on the rise," one of them said. "I was over there, diverting the water. I heard gears grinding and looked up. Stevens was in the air. Hickson was leaning out over the landing with his arms out. The tractor was moving forward and—"

"That was *after*," the other boy said, shaking his head. "I saw the whole thing. Hickson was reaching out to *grab* him, to *help* him. The tractor just lurched. I swear, it was an accident."

"No way was that an accident," the first boy said. "You saw those two this morning, and who do you think is gonna be in charge now?"

"You can't go around making those claims," the other boy said, his voice rising. "Especially if you didn't see—"

"Calm down," I told them. "None of this is going to help. We don't need to spread divisive rumors, okay?"

One of the boys nodded. The other shook his head, but it seemed to be more out of an unwillingness to accept the coincidence than anything else. He let the matter go, and the two turned away from each other, going back to their duties, probably with a mind of seeding their individual version of events among the other colonists.

When I turned back, I saw Tarsi and Kelvin clinging to one another, both looking at the body. We had already begun burying the more than four hundred dead from the previous day, but this one would be different. This would be someone we knew, however briefly. More chilling was that with Stevens's passing, we would be reducing our number by one.

And burying a bit of our hope along with him.

5

FUNERAL

OLIVER INSISTED HIS PROFESSION MADE HIM THE expert on funerals, but none of what he said at the service made any sense to me. He recited memorized passages with an odd syntax, his voice rising and falling theatrically. There was a lot of thanking and rejoicing and talk of Stevens living on in some other place. It made for an uncomfortable scene, especially with most of us fidgeting in our new wardrobes.

The supply group had stitched together pants and tops from the headliners of the tractors and the sound-dampening fabric stapled to the engine compartments. While the material was more pliable than the canvas, it was also itchy and abrasive. I scratched my thigh while one of the dozers pushed dirt over the grave we had lowered Stevens into, a hole apart from the nearby pits of ash and bone. The machine roared noticeably louder than it had the day before—with us now wearing the fabric that had once lined its hood—almost loudly enough to drown out the sniffles from the crowd and Myra's heart-wrenching sobs.

I watched Hickson as the hole gradually became a mound. He seemed suitably distraught until I followed his gaze and realized his dour expression was aimed at Myra and her weeping, and not the grave before her.

After the funeral, we ate the same thing we'd had for lunch: a paste made from the green fruit that fell from the canopy above, washed down with bowls of boiled water. It was hard to judge the taste of the fruit, having never really eaten anything else in my life, but the fact that I looked forward only to sating the grumbling in my stomach surely said something. We ate out of necessity rather than desire, which was not what I knew of hunger.

There was talk of venturing out in the coming days to search for meat, but Colony was being extremely secretive about what we might find. And with the vat module half-ruined and scavenged for supplies, it would be a very long time before we could raise what few Earth animal blastocysts had survived the fires.

"I don't think Myra wants the job of leading us," I heard Tarsi tell Kelvin between bites of paste. I pushed the rest of mine away and drank from one of the many gold bowls the construction crew had stamped out for us. We were arranged in several clusters, each group sitting around raised sheets of gold alloy that served as tables.

"I don't think she should *have* to lead us," Kelvin said. "Not if she doesn't want to."

"We should vote on it," another at our table said.

"Colony is in charge," someone reminded us. "Let it decide who's next in line."

Kelvin reached across and rapped his knuckles on the bright surface in front of me. When I looked up, he asked me, quietly: "What are our chances?"

"For what?" I asked.

He looked around. Our entire table had fallen silent. Everyone shifted their gazes back and forth between us. Amid all the noisy banter, a whisper had somehow caught everyone's attention.

"For *surviving*," Kelvin said. "For making it long term. For not ending up like Stevens."

We all end up like Stevens, I thought to myself. I looked around the

table and considered taking another sip of my water, but knew how in-
decisive that would seem.

"That depends on us," I said. "It depends mostly on how well we
work together. We have enough of a mix of people—both for skills
and producing offspring—that I can see us making it."

I tried to say it like I really believed it, but the truth was: only Colony knew. The most damning evidence was the half-melted remains of
so many of our modules, some of them still smoking. The AI wouldn't
have made that decision lightly. Deep down, I couldn't help but feel
we were just playing a game, hoping to survive long enough to discover
why this planet had been determined to be unviable and pass that information along.

"It's the minerals," Mica said from the other end of the table, almost
as if reading my mind.

I looked at her past all the somber faces. She held my gaze as the
chatter among the diners resumed, everyone drowning each other out.
Her eyes dropped to her hands.

"What do you mean?" I asked her, raising my voice to be heard.

She glanced up at me, then peered down into her bowl, which she
gently cradled in both hands. "This metal is too soft," she said, holding the bowl up for emphasis. "You don't build stuff out of this unless
there's nothing else."

We stared at each other while those between us continued to argue
over our chances of survival.

"Two weeks, max," I heard someone say.

Mica and I continued to stare at one another. Her face was expres-
sionless, none of the worry and crinkled brow everyone else wore. She
looked very matter-of-fact.

I fought to remember what her profession was; she had mentioned
it earlier that morning.

"I give the rocket even worse odds," someone said.

I saw Mica frown. Then I remembered: she had introduced herself
as a geologist.

6

THE ROCKET

THE ROCKET GREW RIGHT ON THE LAUNCH PAD, AS if planted there by a seed. A giant cylinder of steel amid a lattice of scaffolding. Tanks from the fuel depot had been converted into the body. They were split open, some of their plates had been removed, and then the rest was welded back into a tighter cylinder. Several of the other tanks had been converted to store the liquid oxygen and hydrogen that would propel it into orbit. These propellant tanks had been buried to help insulate them and were lined with refrigerant pipes.

Over the next week, I learned more engineering science over meals of green paste than I figured could be crammed into a month of training modules. Still, as I watched sparks fly from cutting torches, and the column grew ever higher, no part of me thought the thing would ever fly. How could it? It was being built by teenage refugees.

Besides, our enthusiasm for the project waned steadily after Stevens died. Hickson had taken over for enforcing Colony's will and did so in a manner that demanded more—and thus received less. Already, I could see people shirking duties to steal a nap or idle away their time. It was a psychological failing I knew well from my studies and was beginning to recognize in myself. One night, lying on the hood of the tractor that had become our official home, Kelvin, Tarsi, Oliver, and I talked about it.

"It's the free rider problem," I told Tarsi, who couldn't understand how the efforts to survive could decline even as the need grew stronger.

"The *what?*" Oliver asked.

"Free rider," I said, turning to him. "It's a problem in game theory, one of the last things I was learning for my profession."

Kelvin laughed. "For all we know, you would've found out a year from now that some other theory proved that one all wrong."

Tarsi slapped him playfully in my defense, since she and Oliver were between us. I dropped the matter, assuming nobody cared, and tried to enjoy the warmth of the overworked engine as it soaked into my back.

"Aren't you going to finish?" Tarsi asked.

I cleared my throat. "Well, the problem arises when people figure out they can take a little more than they're putting in and nobody will notice. It makes sense, actually, for each individual to think this, but when everybody does it, you run into problems."

"How do you stop it?" Tarsi asked.

"Hypnotherapy," Kelvin said.

All of us laughed except for Oliver, who had turned to the side, expecting a real answer from me.

"I have no idea," I admitted. "I think one of the guys in my group has some economics training. He might know. All I know is resentment theory, which deals with people like us."

"Those of us overworked and bitching?" Kelvin asked.

"Pretty much."

Tarsi stood up and stretched, groaning with exhaustion. She had her bottoms on, but had been using her top as a pillow. I watched her body elongate as she reached to the sky and arched her back. I noticed the way her ribs had become more and more visible. We were all losing weight, but some of us had started with less to begin with.

"I'm going to use the bathroom and turn in," she said. "Anyone else need to go?"

Oliver stood without a word, and the two of them moved off together. One of the strange things I had noticed about Oliver over the past few days was how severe his swings in mood were. One minute, the worst events were causing him to assuage us, telling us it was the will of the gods and part of a plan greater than we could know. Other times—when tragedy was in the back of most of our minds—he became sullen and almost what I would diagnose as clinically depressed. I kept meaning to make time to speak with him, to see how he was doing, but the leisure time for even snippets of conversation seemed hard to come by. Every hour of our days was meticulously planned for us.

After the two of them left, Kelvin slid over next to me. He interlocked his hands behind his head, leaving his elbows pointing up toward the canopy.

"What's the story between you and Tarsi?" he asked.

"The story?"

"The deal. Are you guys—is there anything there?"

I propped myself up on my side and pulled his elbow down so I could see him. The light from the cab spilled through the glass behind us, illuminating his face with a dull glow. The flat planes of his skull and his strong brow were highlighted by harsh shadows and low-slanting rays.

"What are you talking about?" I asked. "You're the one who sleeps beside her every night."

"I'm just asking because—well, I see how you guys are. I just wanted to know before anything happened and one of us had our feelings hurt. And look, I'm being practical as well. We're a year out before our numbers start going up, you know what I mean?"

I flopped to my back, looking up through the canopy for a fleeting glimpse of a star. Somewhere in the distance, one of the local fruit whistled through the air and struck something metal with a loud crack. People had already begun calling them bombfruit for the sound they made as they plummeted from so great a height. As if any of us had ever heard a real bomb before.

"I don't feel that way about her," I finally said. And saying it, I realized I meant it. I *didn't* feel that way about her. It felt like family, nothing more. Well, could anything be *more* than family? Maybe it felt like family, nothing *less*.

Now, Stevens . . . I think I had felt that way for him. I closed my eyes and tried to feel differently, certain some training module had been missed. In all my couples therapy modules, it'd been a male-and-a-female simulated couple. I'd never seen anything else. And yet . . .

"Mica's more your type, isn't she?" Kelvin asked. He elbowed me in the ribs, chuckling.

"Yeah," I lied. "She's more my type." I sat up, the heat from the engine compartment no longer soothing against my back. "I'll see you in the morning," I said, hurrying off to bed.

For some reason, my entire body burned as I went, my face feeling as if it were on fire.

7

COLONY

A FEW MORNINGS LATER, I MADE MY FIRST MAJOR mistake, one that would alter the course of our little colony for the worse. Our foursome had stayed up late the night before, bemoaning the progress on the rocket, the mission package, and the infrastructure needed for long-term survival. We came to a conclusion: the moment Stevens had died, everything had changed. Tarsi told us how Hickson had the supply group scavenging more for parts than food. Kelvin pinpointed Stevens's demise as the moment the construction group found themselves pulled off farming and moved solely to propellants.

Hickson had begun misallocating our energy — sapping what remained of it in the process. I had become lazier myself, concentrating more on how hard my neighbor worked or how much the person across from me consumed at dinner rather than looking to my own labors or my own plate. Maybe it was my training bias. I had been pulled out of — and was therefore permanently stuck in — the late twentieth Earth century. I knew from that era's experiments that we would all be dead before the rocket was complete if we continued down our current path.

So I decided to take action. Later that morning, I went to have a talk with Colony.

I found Myra at the door of the command module. She and a few others from that first night had taken up residence in the structure. Hickson had moved in after Stevens died; rumor even had it that his handful of belongings had showed up *before* the funeral.

As I approached, I noticed how tired Myra looked. From what little I knew of her, I had a hard time imagining how she could cohabitate with the guy presently running our colony into the ground. She attempted a smile by way of greeting but couldn't quite manage it.

"How're you holding up?" I asked her.

"Fine," she said, nodding her head. "Hickson's not here, if that's who you're after."

"Hickson? I've got nothing to say to him. Why would you think I came for him?"

"Oh. He told me he really needed to speak with you." She looked past me toward the cluster of modules and parked tractors. "Must've crossed paths."

"I came to see how you were doing, see if you wanted to come spend a night with us. We have a little group that sleeps in a construction tractor." I turned and pointed. In the distance I could see Tarsi and Kelvin still out on the hood. "We talk at night, and I just thought—"

"I know where you sleep," Myra said. I turned back around and saw her shaking her head. "I can't. It wouldn't feel right—"

"What? No!" I laughed and shook my head. "No, not like that. I'm a psychologist. If you need to talk, well, forget my profession, if you just need any friends—"

"I have my group here," she said. "I'm Hickson's girl now."

It isn't often one experiences true speechlessness. Not wordlessness, the inability to come up with the right thing to say, but a moment of absolute muteness. Throat constricting, lungs inoperable, mouth dry, jaw unhinged. Truly unable to speak, even knowing what I wanted to say. Or shout.

Myra seemed to hear it all. She shrugged. "He makes me feel safe," she said. "And it meant not having to learn to sleep somewhere else.

Anyway, I'm starting to see those first few days as a training program. My final one. That was the life — minus the grief and the shock — that I'm supposed to work toward. To eventually have. So that's what I'm doing. I'm trying to feel like that again."

"Were — you and Stevens, you were *together* those first days?"

Myra nodded and wiped at her eyes. "It was just training," she whispered.

I grabbed her shoulders and pulled her close to me, wrapping my arms around her. But I could feel her own arms between us, the hard bone from elbow to wrist lined up vertically in front of her chest like bars in a protective fence. Or perhaps a restrictive cage. I held her and tried to comfort her, but just ended up disgusting myself. If an embrace could feel like molestation, that one certainly did. I was wrapping up a thing that didn't want to be touched, so I let her go.

"I need to speak with Colony," I said. I stepped past her and into the command module, shaking my head with the shame of the encounter.

Behind me, her voice cracked as she tried to argue — to say I wasn't allowed — but I heard her resistance crumble before she could even erect it, the squeak of her voice like the last wail of something dying within her.

And in those uncomfortable, tragic moments, Myra had perfectly demonstrated why I had come to speak with Colony. She was moving through a deteriorating progression, the will to live leaching out through her pores. She had arrived at the last stages of some disassembly line, one we all were traveling down and couldn't seem to get off.

I sat in the center seat, directly in front of the main monitor. Doing so reminded me of Stevens, and I had a brief terror of sullying the spot, until I remembered who probably spent a good bit of his time in it now. Again, I thought of Myra and felt the imaginary belt beneath us move several feet, taking me further down that line.

"Colony?"

"Hello, Porter," the computer said. It was the same calm and collected voice of my training, of my simulated childhood—the same voice that had soothed me that first night in the command module. Now the calm in its voice just made me angry. The lack of urgency seemed like an absence of feeling, rather than the possession of some inner strength.

I gripped the edge of the table, trying to maintain my balance, to remember why I had come. "Colony, we have some problems around base."

"I am well aware of that, Porter, and I am working hard to correct them. We should be able to resume production at the tank facility this afternoon. A revised timetable will be posted by your group coordinator."

"I'm sure it will, Colony, but I wanted to talk to you about why those production revisions need to be drawn up every day. And it isn't this planet's limited ore supply."

"If you have a theory, I would be more than happy to entertain it."

"Of course, that's why I came to you. I think it—we think, some colonists and I—that the more we focus on the construction of the rocket and the less we concentrate on basic needs, the more we're getting behind on both."

"You believe this is a question of morale," Colony said.

"I—well, yes! I have several psychological arguments planned, if you'd like to hear them."

"Porter." Colony paused, leaving my name hanging in the air. *"Who taught you what you know of psychology?"*

I sat, dumbfounded for a moment, before dropping my head and peering down at the keyboard in front of me. Lines of fire retardant were still stuck between each key, and dirty smudges could be seen on the desk where someone's palms had been resting.

"You did," I whispered, feeling like a complete fool.

"I sense humiliation, which was not my intent. I had merely hoped to

save you the time in arguing, time that could be better spent in produc-tion."

I nodded. I understood the logic but still felt miserable inside. I ac-tually could feel my energy to work being sapped away as a depression grew, fueled by a sense of worthlessness.

"I appreciate your coming by, Porter. You are a valuable member of this colony."

"Thanks," I said, about as lifeless and sincere as the computer's voice.

I stood up and began to walk away, when the computer said: *"Por-ter."*

"Yeah?" I asked, turning.

"I will make some changes. Starting today."

"Thanks," I said, feeling grateful.

Albeit, prematurely.

I made my way back through the tight passage between the servers and into the wide space full of bedrolls. Someone stomped up the ramp outside, and I tried to think of what I wanted to say to Myra—when Hickson burst through the door and nearly ran me over.

"What the hell are you doing in here?" he asked.

"I came to speak with Colony," I said, looking back over my shoul-der for emphasis. Before I could turn back, Hickson had both hands on my shoulders. He pushed me across someone's bedroll and against the wall.

"Nobody speaks to Colony but me, do you understand?"

I tried to focus on his face, but it was too close to my own. It was a wall of angered red flesh filling my vision. I nodded slightly, worried our noses might collide. "I was just trying to—"

"I don't care *what* you were trying to do," Hickson said, letting go of me and stepping back. He positioned himself between me and the servers. "Get out."

Gladly, I thought, moving toward the door. When I got there, I saw Myra sitting at the end of the ramp, her chin in her hands. It reminded me of something. Stepping back through the door, I called after Hickson, who had already started back through the servers.

"Hey, did you want to see me about something?"

Hickson turned halfway around. He rested a hand on the server in front of him and leaned his forehead against the back of his hand. He stood like that for a minute, and I started to ask him again, when he spoke.

"No," he said. "It's nothing. Forget about it."

Not likely, I thought. I stepped around Myra and out into the clearing, thinking about how I was going to always remember that exchange.

8

TREMORS

I LEFT THE COMMAND MODULE AND HEADED TO-ward the mess tent, where I hoped to find anything other than fruit paste for breakfast. That was when the first tremors began.

At first, I thought the rumbling was emanating from my stomach. Usually, the growling turned into a hollow ache, a silent sort of cramping, like my intestines were tying themselves in knots. But this time, it kept growing louder. Then the ground moved beneath my feet, and a nauseating sensation overtook me as my inner ear and my legs disagreed on how to remain upright.

I threw my arms out and fell into a low, wide stance, as several other colonists on their way to breakfast did the same. In the part of my brain that knew vocabulary words with no real context, I realized we were experiencing an earthquake. I knew it like I knew what air was, what trees were, with no deeper understanding beyond the mere concept. I thought if we all stayed put, it would go away and everything would be fine.

Then I heard the whistling.

The first bombfruit smacked the ground not ten feet in front of me. The whistling grew louder and more menacing as the sounds seemed to come from everywhere at once. A dozen more of the skull-sized fruit struck the earth all around me, some of them exploding in a shower of fragmented rind and tossing seeds and fruit meat into the air.

I ran for the mess tent, shifting side to side as the ground continued to vibrate beneath me. When I saw one of the bombfruit slice right through the fabric of the tent and explode on one of the metal tables, I changed course, sprinting toward the old vat module instead.

A dozen other colonists had the same idea. A girl ahead of me was nearly taken out by one of the fruit; it exploded in front of her and she went down, slipping in the meat. I stopped to help her up, and we both nearly collapsed as a large tremor rippled through the solid rock. We scurried forward, trying to reach the others inside the module, and finally crashed through the doorway and tripped over those already inside.

All of us pushed our way deeper into the module to make room for those coming behind. It was a bizarre re-creation of our birthday, but played out in reverse—we packed ourselves in among the vats, seeking safety in the place we had once fled.

Numerous strikes landed on the roof above with enough force to hurt our ears. We cringed in unison each time, but the waiting between the strikes was even worse. The anticipation would draw out our nerves into thin wires, and then the next bombfruit would pluck them.

Our little group settled in, hugging our shins and one another. People wondered how long it would last, as if any of our guesses had merit. We hoped aloud that the other colonists had found shelter as well.

During a lull in the vibrations, I left the girl I had helped and made my way back toward the door, needing to see what was going on outside. Before I got there, Kelvin staggered through, his arm around Tarsi, both of them covered in blood.

I ran forward, cursing, not sure which of them to grab. Tarsi looked up, her eyes wide and full of fear. "Help," she mouthed, the sound of her voice cut off by another strike above.

Kelvin practically fell into my arms. I lowered him to the decking as gently as I could. Half his face was covered in blood. I reached for his neck, recalling my first aid and mumbling to myself as I tried to remember whether we should be elevating his head or his feet.

"Sit him up," another colonist said, coming over to help. I was pretty sure she was right. A few of us struggled with Kelvin's arms; we dragged him back against a vat. He seemed to weigh a ton. I ran my hands over his head, searching for the wound, and my palms came away sticky with fruit meat and blood.

Kelvin's eyes opened briefly, flickered, then widened. They rolled around, unfocused, as he blinked rapidly. "Where am I?" he asked.

Someone passed me their shirt, and I began wrapping it around Kelvin's head. "You're okay," I said. "Just rest."

"I feel shaky," he told me.

"That's the ground," Tarsi said. She grabbed my arm and scooted closer to us both. "What's going on?" she asked me. "Is this an earth-quake?"

I nodded. "I think so."

Even as we discussed it, the rumbles seemed to fade away, almost as if receding into the distance. The whistles and strikes continued for a few more minutes, but none of us ventured outside until they had ceased completely.

After what felt like half an hour with no whistles, we exited the module to find the rest of the colonists staggering from their own chosen shelters, all of us marveling at the level of destruction and the green fruit meat that littered the ground.

Out of habit, or time of day, or maybe the sight of so much food, we coalesced around the mess tent—or what was left of it. I went to get some water out of one of the gold rain barrels to wash Kelvin's wound when Oliver came running up, a red-topped blur of excitement.

"Did you see it?" he asked me.

"See what, the shit storm of bombfruit? Everyone saw it."

"It was a miracle," Oliver said, his face dead serious. "A miracle."

I reached deep into the water barrel with my bowl; the level had lowered due to a direct hit from a bombfruit, which rested, intact, at the bottom. "I need to tend to Kelvin," I told Oliver. "I don't have time for this."

"But don't you see?" He tugged on my arm. "You went to Colony because the people had grown hungry, and what happened?" He spread his arms. "Manna from the gods," he whispered.

"Yeah, well, the gods have good aim. See if you can find some clean rags—Kelvin's head nearly got split open."

Oliver clapped his hands together and ran off. I watched him as I made my way back to my friends, but he didn't go looking for a rag or anything practical. Instead, I saw him tugging on others, pointing toward the command module and up at the sky, spreading talk of gods and of our salvation.

9

THE GOLDEN BULLET

FOR THE REST OF THAT DAY, THE GROUND AND MY stomach remained thankfully quiet. The grumblings among the colonists, however, didn't seem to abate. The calories from the bombfruit were worked off with complaining, rather than being focused on the tasks at hand. I heard more than one person question why they were wasting their time on a rocket when more important things needed doing, and I realized I needed to speak with Colony again.

Before I could work out how to get around Hickson to do that, Kelvin came to me at dinner with another, far more serious problem. He plopped down on the ground across from me, his bandaged head hanging low. I was about to ask him how he was feeling when his hand slid across the table toward me.

Just as I looked down at it, the hand pulled away, leaving behind a single golden bullet.

"Where did you get this?" I asked. I knew immediately what it was —just as I knew an earthquake.

"I made it," he said flatly.

"Why?" I looked up at him, wondering what procedures I'd missed in the concussion analysis tests I had him perform over lunch.

"Hickson pulled me off farm detail. All of us, in fact. The tractors are no longer allowed to be used for anything. Anyway, two other construction guys are in a room we converted in the tool module. I haven't seen what they're making, but I saw the pipes going in, and I had someone ask me about rifling barrels."

"They're making *guns?*" I asked, my voice as low as I could make it and still be heard.

Kelvin nodded.

Oliver and Tarsi walked up with two of the support people I recognized but didn't know very well. My hand immediately covered the bullet. I slid it off the table and into my lap, reminding myself for the third or fourth time that day that I needed to sew a few pockets into my new garments.

"You boys look serious," Tarsi said. She jerked her head my way. "If you're thinking of changing your earlier diagnosis, I should warn you that he wasn't too bright to begin with."

She smiled at Kelvin, who smirked and scrunched up his face for effect. "Actually," he said, "we were just arguing over who should have to sleep on the floor tonight."

"It's *our* night," she said, scooping up some fresh fruit paste with one of the bright yellow spoons.

"Yeah," Oliver said. "My back can't take two nights in a row on the floor."

"No," Kelvin said, his face still creased with sarcasm and false hurt. "I was just telling Porter that it's no fair I've had to sleep with you every night, and that *he* should have to take a turn."

Tarsi put down her spoon and turned to me.

"He's just playing with you," I told her. "I never said that."

"I'll take a turn," Oliver said, digging into his paste and watching Tarsi out of the corner of his eye.

Tarsi glared at me, her eyes angry slits.

"What?" I asked. "I swear, he's just getting you back for calling him dumb just now."

"We'll talk about this later," she said, turning back to her bowl.

"Yeah." I looked across at Kelvin and held up my closed fist, the cool cylinder of gold wrapped up inside it. "We'll talk about this later," I whispered.

That night, the three of us lounged on the hood of our tractor, recuperating from another day of impossible deadlines. For the first time, the metal surface was as cool as the night, as nothing had been done on the farms all day. It was also our first night without Oliver.

His absence made it feel like a wheel had been removed from our home, our little family now unbalanced and incomplete. He had come by earlier to get a few of his things and to explain his desire to sleep closer to the command module. It had been an awkward moment, none of us knowing what to say. It almost felt as if we would never see each other again, even though the lone window of the command module could be seen from our hood, and he had promised to join us at every meal.

So the three of us lay in an unusual cool silence. Kelvin and Tarsi continued pretending to be mad at each other; a series of jabs and jokes earlier in the day had somehow turned into a spat of sorts. It designated me the third wheel, even as Tarsi forced me to scoot over and lie in the middle. She snuggled up to me, but I couldn't help but sense it was an assault on Kelvin more than a true gesture of affection.

For a brief moment, I imagined Kelvin sidling up against my other side to return the blow, and the visual imagery excited me . . . sexually. Then it filled me with shame. I concentrated on making my arousal go away, which just made it throb all the stronger. Looking down my body, I could see the swelling in my pants illuminated from the glow of the tractor's cab. I felt like my two friends could see it as well, but I worried that covering it would just draw more attention. The more I thought about it, the more my erection grew, until I felt like I was going to die from the humiliation.

"Is there something you want to talk about?" Kelvin asked me.

"What?" I felt my cheeks flush. "I—What would I want to talk about?"

"You know," he said, elbowing me.

"No." I could feel myself turning bright red, but at least the rush of blood put an end to the source of my embarrassment. "I have no idea what you're referring to," I said.

"The bullet," he whispered.

Oh. I exhaled. "Yeah," I said.

"What bullet?" Tarsi asked loudly. She rolled on her side and draped one of her knees across my legs, resting her chin on my chest.

"Shhh," Kelvin hissed. "Voices carry out here."

He wasn't kidding. A few nights earlier we'd spent our entire time on the hood giggling, the four of us wrapped together in fits of hysteria while two other colonists sat on top of the power module and told each other how madly in love they were.

In at least a thousand different ways.

And not all of them verbal.

Tarsi scooted up my body, her knee pressing into my thigh, her lips hovering just a few inches from my cheek.

"What bullet?" she whispered, the air from her lungs tickling the tiny hairs deep inside my ear.

I pushed her away, giggling and digging a finger in my ear after her question, trying to stop it from itching. "Tell her," I told Kelvin.

He quietly related his day's activities, telling us both what the rest of his group had been up to. I sat up, crossed my legs, and turned to face him. By the time he was done, we were all three sitting close together, our heads bent down over our laps. Tarsi looked back and forth between us, her eyebrows low in worry.

"Aren't you two being a little paranoid?" she whispered.

"Paranoid?" Kelvin asked. "They're making *guns,*" he hissed.

"Maybe to go hunting. Or for defense," Tarsi said.

"Then why make them in secret?" I asked her.

"They aren't. *We're* the ones making them."

Kelvin shook his head. "I don't know. You had to see how it was being done. Everyone was kept apart, and nobody is talking about it."

"*We're* talking about it," Tarsi said. "And everything is being done that way. Building the rocket, waking us up, preparing for the future. I think you guys are reading too much into this." She pointed to Kelvin. "You, I understand." She jabbed a finger at me. "When did *you* get bonked on the head?"

"I think he's right," I told her. "And I think maybe it's all my fault."

"*Your* fault? How is that?" Tarsi asked.

Kelvin looked to me as well. I tried to sort out how to put it, but the theory had just begun to form while listening to Tarsi's doubts.

"I think it might have something to do with the conversation I had with Colony this morning."

Kelvin frowned. "I thought you said that went well."

"Yeah," Tarsi said. "According to Oliver, it brought about a 'miracle.'"

I frowned at her. "Colony said it was going to change some things. I thought it meant we would get back to planning for the future and chill out on the rocket schedule, maybe give morale a boost."

"How does making guns help that?" Tarsi asked.

"It doesn't," I said. I glanced back and forth between them. "Unless you decide you don't give a fuck about morale."

We stared at one another in silence, unbroken until the whistle of a bombfruit descended from the canopy, causing us to tense up, fearful of the impact. It had become our normal reaction to the sound ever since the tremors. A sign, perhaps, of our growing learned sense of helplessness.

10

ORDER

I HAD MORE NIGHTMARES THAT NIGHT — THE WORST ones yet. In one, it wasn't bombfruit falling from the trees, but the heads of the 400-plus colonists who hadn't made it out of the vat module. They rained down on us, streaming fire, and landed charred and black but still screaming. We gathered them up from the ground and ate them raw, lapping at the stuff spilling from the cracked skulls, caring more about our survival than the foul taste. And in the dream, I knew it wouldn't be long before we ran out of heads and those of us left alive would turn on each other.

A few days later, shadows of these dreams leaked out into the real world as a new group formed. The first person I saw with a gun on his side wasn't Hickson, as I expected it to be — it was Oliver. Not that he got his weapon first; I just wasn't actively avoiding him the way I was Hickson and some of the others.

I passed him on my way to the power module, where I was helping build the mission package. The bright golden object gleamed from his hip and captured my attention. He greeted me, but I couldn't hear what he said. I was distracted by the sight of him carrying something I knew, even if only from training modules, to be very dangerous.

"I said good afternoon," Oliver repeated.

I nodded, looked up, and tried my best to return his smile. "Missed you at lunch," I said. "And the floor of the tractor gets pretty cold without you there."

Oliver frowned. "Yeah, weird how I miss sleeping like that. But I've moved into the command module full-time. Hickson made me an enforcer. No more bombfruit duty for me, scraping up all that green mess."

"An enforcer?" I asked. "What's that?"

"We've been falling more and more off schedule. The enforcers make sure we get back on track." He raised a finger and twirled it in a large circle above his head. "We've got floodlights going up today so we can work later into the evening. And with the gift we received the other day, nobody should go hungry as we wrap up this project."

"Wrap it up?" I asked. "Don't we need to be thinking about the long haul? Where's the power for these floodlights gonna come from? We're rationing energy here in the very module that's supposed to make it."

"We're cutting juice back from the security perimeter. There hasn't been any sign of predators—" Oliver stopped and looked me up and down. "Jeez, Porter, you sound pretty tense. Is everything all right? Do you need some spiritual guidance to get you through these dark times?"

I laughed, then felt bad for doing so as I saw a spasm of pain in Oliver's cheeks. "No," I said. "I'm fine. I just— I guess some of us are finding it hard to sacrifice so much for a project we aren't really being told anything about."

Oliver nodded. "I understand," he said. "You scientists are always the first to become doubters."

"It isn't that, it's just—"

Oliver raised his hand. "I'm here to talk, to help you, but not to listen. I don't want you filling my head with any . . . *whatever*—" He turned to go.

"Oliver, wait. I didn't mean to—"

He turned, his face twisted up in an expression of pure rage that brought me to a halt. "Colony gave you *life*," he spat. "Don't you understand that? It taught you everything you know. None of us would even be here without it. If everything had gone perfectly, if there were a half thousand of us clearing these lands and breeding like animals, would you question your existence then? Would you curse the person who made you and taught you how to live your life? Or would you carry on building yourself a better world in the service of Colony and country?"

"I don't see—"

"I know you don't, Porter. You don't see what's going on. No matter what happens here, some of us have it in our hearts to obey, and some have the compulsion to rebel. I bet if I were telling you to farm these lands, you would be out building yourself a rocket. We should probably be using some of that—oh, what do you call it?"

"Reverse psychology?"

"Yeah, some of that." Oliver jabbed his finger at me. "You know, you've been miserable since the day we were born, and that's probably your lot in life, but not me. I know the glory of the gods, and I for one will work in their service. I've been an enforcer of *that* since day one, with or without this," he said, slapping at the gun on his waist.

"You need to search your heart," Oliver told me. "Figure out what you're working toward. Get right with the gods."

He turned and stormed off.

I just watched him go, feeling sorry for him. Then damning him for assaulting me the way he had. For planting a seed of doubt . . .

That night provided the first glimpse of our new life, in all the harshness of 10,000-watt bulbs. After dinner, we were ordered back to our stations to work until we met the day's quota. For our group, that meant finishing the three firing rocket phases attached to the end of the payload body. In order to get the package wherever it was going, three separate canisters full of two-part propellant would need to fire before dropping away. Those of us not really qualified to consider our-

selves "scientists" worked on that, while another group soldered together the circuits that made up the navigation array.

While we worked, one of the guys who used to be with construction—a big lad I'd seen Kelvin speak to during meals—stood by the
door, one hand resting on his gun. It was strange how readily we just
went along with his presence, most of us publicly accepting the new
rules with a shrug, only to complain and moan once nobody could
hear. Muriel, the girl helping me plumb the mixing valves for each of
the three tanks, slept in the same module as the guy enforcing us. Several times, she tried to strike up a conversation, asking him how he was
enjoying his new job, but he never replied. What little joy there was in
our payload group—the jokes and gossip that gave us a tune to work
by—had been sucked right out of the power module, sapped like the
energy being diverted from the defense grid to feed the demanding
lights.

So we worked in a silence punctuated by the occasional grunt of
frustration from someone in our group. Every now and then, a bombfruit whistled outside and all of us cringed in fear. Even though there
was a roof overhead to protect us.

11

THE BREAK

IT'S AMAZING HOW QUICKLY YOU GET USED TO things. My head was full of an education on how to help brains on the verge of breaking, but all I'd seen around me was them bending more and more under a growing strain and somehow remaining whole. For all the studying I'd done on the fragility of a thing, here I was a witness and example of its incredible perseverance.

Another thing I noticed was how quickly the human brain paired causal events. "A" leads to "B." We love to make that link, however tenuous. Like how Tarsi hits people when she's joking. As soon as she slaps someone, you can expect her odd little laugh to follow. The one event follows the other like clockwork. Kelvin and I make fun of the habit, telling her we aren't going to laugh on command anymore. That's why we think she does it, like a little threat of violence if we don't find the last thing she said humorous.

Still, the harder we try not to laugh, the more we end up doing it. Harder and more often of late, it seemed, despite the longer days and the less time we spent together. More evidence of our bending without breaking.

The whistle of the bombfruit was another of those causal pairs. After the whistle, there was usually a bang. Often, it was the softer thud of the rind exploding as it hit the mud, the dirt mixing with our next meal. But sometimes, it was the booming report of a large bombfruit hitting something metal. The next day, a dining group might find a new dent in their gold table, and breakfast already spread out, dutifully tended to by a variety of little worms.

Whistle followed by explosion. Like clockwork. There was always the warning of the first before the bang of the latter. The in-between time was spent tensed up, waiting.

My nerves, then, were not prepared when the sounds reversed themselves. It was late at night, and my group was struggling along to meet its quota. Several of us worked outside joining pipes—not just to keep the fumes of our welding irons away from the others, but because of the ironic state of our lighting. The bulbs outside burned brighter than the dim flickering *within* the power module, which struggled to keep up with demand.

The explosion came without warning. A loud boom. My entire body twitched, and I dropped my iron. We all looked at each other, wondering what had happened. Then the high-pitched screaming started. The two noises had come in the wrong order.

I left my iron in the dirt and ran toward the source, trying to keep up with Muriel, who had taken off immediately.

The wail emanated from the direction of the launch pad. Other colonists converged on it as well, despite the shouts from enforcers to return to our stations. One of them raised his gun and fired a shot straight up.

I cringed, then I realized the sound from the gun was the same as the one we'd heard earlier. The whistling noise was distant shrieks, which grew louder as we stumbled down the slope toward the rocket site.

Several enforcers stood together, their gleaming guns drawn. Hickson came running up to join them, shouting questions. Stephany, one of the girls I knew through Kelvin, sat in the dirt, screaming. She held someone in her lap—an eerie re-creation of what I'd come upon the day Stevens died. The boy was large and unmoving, and for a second I thought it was Kelvin, but then I saw him drop down from the scaffolding.

"What did you *do?*" Stephany shrieked, rocking back and forth. I ran to her, joining Julie—a nurse who had become, by default, the base's doctor.

The boy had both hands pressed to his stomach, vainly attempting to stanch the flow of blood. His chest heaved in and out rapidly; the only other things moving were his eyes, which darted back and forth between us.

"Let me see," Julie said, pulling his hands away and pushing the thin fabric of his top up to his chest. Blood welled out, thick and dark; she immediately placed her hands over the wound and started barking out commands: water, clean towels, coagulant. I didn't hear what else. Someone pulled me back forcefully.

"Give them room," Hickson said.

I stumbled backwards, feeling a fury rise up inside. One of the enforcers came to me, holding the gun out between us, but he wasn't threatening me with it. He held it limp and on its side, looking at it like he wasn't sure how it got there.

"I didn't mean to—" he said. He looked at me, water coating his eyes. "He was trying to take an extra break," he told me. "I didn't mean to—"

I pushed the gun down, getting the barrel away from me, and looked around for Kelvin. He stood beside the scaffolding, his fists clenched in front of him, his eyes glaring daggers at Hickson.

I stepped away from the enforcer, leaving him to him cope with his guilt alone, and ran to my friend to save him from making a huge mistake.

Later that night, the three of us sat together in the cab of our tractor, the overhead light turned up just enough so we wouldn't bump into each other. It felt hot and muggy inside, but none of us felt safe out on the hood. Partly out of fear of being overheard, and partly out of fear of the bombs overhead.

"We need to get out of here," Kelvin said, looking back and forth between Tarsi and me.

"And go where?" Tarsi asked. "Just wander out into the wilderness of a planet we haven't been properly oriented for? Colony won't even show anyone the satellite maps. We have no idea what's out there."

"We know what's in here," Kelvin said.

"Tarsi's right," I told Kelvin. "Besides, we would just be abandoning everyone else."

"Anyone who wants to come can come," he said. "The more the merrier. The place gets enough rain, right? And there must be tons of bombfruit out there, especially since the tremors. It'll last us until we get started—"

"Started on what?" I asked. "Rubbing sticks together? Do you have any idea how long it would take us to rebuild even a fraction of all this?"

Kelvin squared his shoulders at me and raised his voice. "Do you have any idea how long we'll last here if we keep killing one another?"

"Settle down," Tarsi said. "Both of you."

"I'm sorry," Kelvin said. "I'm just so angry at what happened today. I knew that enforcer was going to do something. We'd been whispering about it all across the scaffolding today. Hell, I should've done something earlier."

"Then *you'd* be the one getting a blood transfusion," Tarsi said, holding his arm with both her hands.

Kelvin sniffed, his mouth tilting up at an angle. He looked to each of us in turn. "You guys can stay here if you want," he said, "but I'm leaving. I'm gonna take a piece of magnesium from the supply store and a machete, so I can start a fire. Maybe a few strips of canvas for carrying water or to make a shelter. Not much. I don't care if I only last a week. But I'm not gonna sit here and watch us tear one another apart."

Before I could complain, Tarsi floored me with her reaction.

"I'll come with you," she said. "I can grab a few seed packets from support in the morning. But I think we should spread the word, give others the chance to join us."

I shook my head at this, arguing tactics when what I should've been doing was dismissing their entire plan. "Tell anyone and you'll be stopped. By force."

"So you're staying," Kelvin said.

"I don't think I can leave," I told them. I immediately recognized the hurt on Tarsi's face. "I'm sorry, it just feels suicidal to me. And I think you guys should sleep on it and reconsider. Give it a day, at least. Once you go, Hickson will know what happened. I don't think you'll be able to come back—"

Saying it cemented the seriousness of what they were considering. I pictured myself sleeping in the tractor at night. Alone. I turned away and pretended to peer through the cab's glass, but it was fogged with a billion droplets of our condensed worry.

"I don't want you guys to go," I whispered. "There's no telling what's beyond our perimeter."

"We'll give it a day," Tarsi said. I felt her turn away from me to face Kelvin. "Is that okay with you? We could use it to gather a few things. Another day like today, and I don't think we'll be alone in going."

"Another day like today, and I won't have any of my sanity left," Kelvin said. "In which case, the shrink here will *have* to come."

Tarsi slapped him in my defense—which automatically got us laughing. It felt nice, even if we weren't sure why we were doing it.

And I don't know that we would've been laughing, had we known it would be the last time the three of us enjoyed a moment like that in our small home. Because, even though Tarsi and Kelvin had agreed to wait a day, we would soon discover that the day would not wait for us.

12

MISSING

FOR THE SECOND STRAIGHT NIGHT, I HARDLY SLEPT a wink. And when I did, more nightmares chased me, nightmares of waking and finding myself alone. Several times, I snuck out and sat on the hood, trying to catch the glimpse of a star through the dense canopy overhead and listening to the occasional whistle of breakfast falling, cringing in anticipation of getting whacked the way Kelvin had.

When the others woke, we performed our morning routine, taking turns with the solar shower hanging from the cab. The water barely warmed up in the filtered sunlight, and what heat it absorbed tended to leak out over the cool evenings. Once again, I resolved to take my showers at night, even though I knew I'd be too exhausted and too eager to spend time with my friends to follow through.

After the shower, my solitary change of clothes went back on, immediately undoing most of my hard-won freshness. The only alteration in our routine that morning was the lack of banter, each of us mulling over decisions that would be impossible to undo once decided upon. We were practicing the *soft* sciences, the fuzzy physics, each of us dreading a collapse into surety.

We walked to breakfast in more silence, took our meager helpings of fruit paste, and sat around peering down at our food and at the scratched and dented surface of our table. We rarely looked at one another during the half hour allotted for meals. As we split up—each of us heading to our duty stations—I heard some grumblings from another table about Mica and Peter not showing up for breakfast. I thought nothing of it at the time.

It was lunchtime before we found out they were missing. Myra came and delivered a message to our enforcer right before break. Whether because of my profession or some sliver of a bond we'd formed in our few tense encounters, she sought me out after delivering her message.

"We need to talk," she said, standing at the end of my workstation.

I finished threading a cap on one of the fuel stages and stood up. "Of course. Are you okay?"

She waved me through the module without a word. Outside, I noticed a lot of people milling about. Either the clock in our module had run down or people were going on break early.

"What is it?" I asked Myra. "Is everything okay with you?"

"It's not me. It's Mica and Peter. They haven't been seen since dinner."

"Last night? And they aren't out on the farm?" I looked off in that general direction, even though the plots of land were over a rise and out of sight.

"They haven't been working out there for days. They were supposed to be helping the support group on the canopy-clearing project."

"The little rockets?"

"Yeah, they should've reported to the tool module for black powder refinement, but they weren't even at breakfast."

I looked past Myra at the activity around camp. The pattern of movement made more sense. People were spreading out. *Searching.*

Myra pushed her short bangs back on her head. "Have you had much contact with them? Seen anything unusual?"

I shook my head. "No, but we're all exhausted. Maybe they're just taking a day off." I tried to make it sound reasonable, but I didn't believe it myself. "Where did they normally sleep?"

"The communications module. But supply works in there during the day. They aren't there."

"Let's head over and take a look," I said. I set off toward the communications module without waiting for her to agree.

"What are you thinking?" Myra asked, hurrying to catch up.

"I'm thinking we might find they aren't the only things missing."

There was only one person working in the module when we arrived. The place had a strong chemical odor as vials of bubbling fluids sent off wisps of dangerous-smelling smoke. Kayla, a girl I had spoken to several times, turned from a makeshift workstation, a crude plastic visor over her face.

"Find them?" she asked Myra. "Oh, hello, Porter."

"Hey. Do you sleep here?"

Kayla shook her head. "I sleep in the power module. Remember? You dripped solder on my bedroll the other day. Found it in my hair during breakfast." She smiled, but it faded quickly as she looked back and forth between us. "Has something bad happened to them?"

"I don't know. I need to find out where they keep their stuff."

"Oh." Kayla stood up and took off her visor, laying it carefully on the workstation. "Mica is in here all the time. I know where she keeps her sack."

We followed her to the end of the module where a wall of shelves had been built by someone in construction. Most of the cubbies were full of labeled golden canisters, but the top shelf was packed with bedrolls and duffels made out of stitched canvas. Kayla stretched up on her tiptoes and moved several of the bags aside.

"That's weird," she said. "She always comes to this corner." She walked down the row of shelves, craning her neck to see up top, but I already knew the answer.

"It's not here," Kayla said.

I nodded, turning to Myra.

"You knew," she said.

"I suspected."

"What is it?" Kayla asked, but Myra was pulling me back to the door and out of the module. I thanked Kayla over my shoulder for her help.

Myra turned to me once we were outside. "You think they left, don't you?"

"I do. I think—"

"Did you see this coming? Why didn't you warn us? Isn't this what your profession does?"

I felt a flush of anger at the accusation and pointed toward the power module. "I build satellites," I said, my voice much louder than I was used to hearing it. "I solder plumbing and I make propulsion stages. I do shit I couldn't have spelled two weeks ago."

Myra ran her hands over her face and looked down at her feet. "I know," she said. "I'm sorry. I— It's been crazy the last week. But if you thought this was a possibility—"

"It never occurred to me until last night," I said, which was the truth. "It was just a fleeting thought, really. I was wondering how long before people broke down, before they mutinied or ran."

"Mutiny?" Myra cocked her head to one side. I watched as her hand came up and rested on her gun, then remembered who she slept with of late. "What have you heard? Is it Kelvin?"

"What? No! I haven't heard anything." I tried to convince her with my eyes, but hers were no longer on me—they were scanning the dispersing crowd, which was searching for the missing couple. "I just worry we're pushing people too hard," I said. "It's just a matter of time before some of us break down."

Myra narrowed her eyes and focused on me again. "We're colonists, Porter. We were trained for this."

That's bullshit, I wanted to say, but I managed to restrain myself. I was beginning to suspect Myra and I were not on the same side. Then it hit me—this series of sickening realizations: Had Mica and Peter not run, had the conversation in the tractor gone differently last night, the base could be having these very conversations about my friends, about Kelvin and Tarsi. I was empathizing with Mica and Peter while Myra was probably thinking about stringing them up for treason.

"I need to go tell Hickson," Myra said. "Go grab a quick lunch and then come to the command module. We need to start searching the perimeter, see if they were able to get through the fence somehow."

I nodded, glad to be done with the conversation.

The perimeter fence had been built on top of a wide berm that ringed the entire base. Soil had been pushed up from both sides fifteen years ago, creating ditches on either side that made the ten-foot electrified fence all the more daunting to predators from without.

And prisoners within.

I stood in the inner ditch with Scott, a construction worker I'd been paired up with for the search. The two of us admired Mica's handi-work. Five of the horizontal bars had been clipped—or more likely, as I examined them closely, they had been melted with acid or a cut-ting torch. Their edges drooped, and the ends were bubbled and un-even. Five insulated wires had been attached to each bar; their coils snaked down into the ditch, leaving plenty of room for someone to crawl through.

It looked like Mica's new electrical training had served her rather than the colony.

"Not bad," Scott said.

"Yeah," I said. I wondered if he was taking notes as well. "Then again, these things weren't built to keep out sentient life. Any of *that* on this planet and we would've been aborted fifteen years ago when it was a lot less messy."

"Gross, Porter." Scott frowned and slapped me on the back. "Let's go tell the others."

"Let's save the walk," I said. I reached out, grabbed one of the insu-lated wires, and jerked it free. The buzzing from the electrified fence shifted in frequency, becoming agitated like a startled hive of bees. In the distance, a horn sounded, whirring up and down from scream to moan and back again. The noise gave me a chill, but I felt satisfied with the little test.

Scott punched me in the arm. I turned to defend my actions, but he just stood there, smiling at me.

"You scientists are fuckin' awesome," he said.

13

COVER

TARSI AND I SAT IN THE CAB OF OUR TRACTOR, alone. Kelvin had to work late on the launch pad, as the first of the canopy-clearing missiles had been moved up the timetable and was scheduled to launch that night. We had asked to watch from the pad shelter, but there were concerns about how much bombfruit would fall after the explosion.

The food, of course, would be a welcome bonus, even if much of it would be wasted. After the tremors, we had learned bombfruit meat didn't stay fresh for long, even with refrigeration. Hairy worms appeared in them after a while, and even though we knew a ton of fruit was rotting on the ground beyond the fence, nobody was allowed outside. With work on the farm halted, the hope around the colony was that the missile would do more than clear a hole for the rocket — it might see us through another week.

"What do you think Mica and Peter are doing right now?" Tarsi asked me.

"I don't know," I said, "but I hope they're able to find some cover."

"Me too. And I hope they found something different to eat."

"That would be nice." I leaned forward and looked up through the glass at the absolute blackness above. "It must grow fast, to have closed us in like this."

"The canopy?"

"Yeah. Don't you think the lander had to burn a hole through it?"

"It's been fifteen years," Tarsi said. "I personally think we should wait and clear the canopy when the rocket's almost done."

"Hickson's pissed," I said. "He needs to blow something up."

"Speaking of pissed, please don't be."

I turned to Tarsi. "What is it?"

"I spoke to Kelvin after dinner. He's dead set on getting out. Maybe tonight."

"And you're going with him?"

Tarsi shook her head. "No. I told him I was staying with you. I begged him to reconsider, and he said he wouldn't go without coming by and seeing us and getting his stuff, but I think he was hoping we would both come."

"And you've changed your mind? Are you sure?"

Tarsi reached out and took my hand with both of hers. She held it in her lap. "I want to be with you," she said.

I nodded, thinking I knew what she meant.

She leaned forward and pressed her lips to mine—showing me I had absolutely no idea what she had meant.

We kissed. I'd seen a few other couples around base do it, and knew of it like I knew of earthquakes, guns, and beehives. But once again, concept gave me a mere glimpse of reality. Actual things kept proving louder and more dangerous than the idea of them.

Our lips moved together and it felt electric, but only for a moment. Then it felt wrong. Incestuous. I thought of Kelvin and pulled away. I held her back, my hands on her shoulders.

"Was I doing it wrong?" she asked, her face a mask of seriousness in the cab's dim glow.

I laughed. "How should I know? I've never done it before."

"But you didn't like it," she said.

"No. I loved it. And I love you." I turned to the side and pulled her close, her head resting on my shoulder. "It's Kelvin," I said.

"There's nothing between us," she told me. "I prefer sleeping with him because I can trust myself with him."

"He really likes you," I said, realizing she had missed my point.

I wondered what my point had been.

"I know." She reached up and stroked my arm, rubbing me from my shoulder to my elbow. It felt even better than the kiss. The comfort and intimacy. The newness and the familiarity. "But I get to decide for me," she said. "And I choose you."

I squeezed her tight, trying to picture the two of us together. As a couple. And it didn't fit in my brain. There was no place to slot it. Familiar doubts surfaced, telling me why the thought of Kelvin made our being together impossible. It wasn't because I was worried about taking Tarsi from him—it was because *she* wasn't *him*.

"I don't want to mess up what we have. The three of us," I said.

"There is no three of us if he leaves tonight and you and I stay behind."

"Do you want to go?"

"Yes, but I want to be with you even more."

The words stabbed at my heart, slicing me with their sweetness and sincerity—crushing me with confusion. I saw no easy way to explain how much I loved her and how it wasn't in the same way. How it probably couldn't *ever* be.

"And if I wanted to go?" I asked.

"I would love that even more."

"What would we do? Wander the wilderness?"

"We'd get away from base. We'd make a shelter, gather food, and grow some Terran stuff. Be free."

"Free," I said. "Sounds like a lot of work, being free."

"Probably more work than we're doing now, but it would all be for ourselves."

She was right, and I knew it. It went to the heart of my conversation with Colony, the talk that had given us guns instead of concessions for our well-being.

"Maybe we could find Mica and Peter," I wondered aloud.

Tarsi shook my arm, practically vibrating in her seat. "So you'll come!" she yelped.

"Yeah," I said, speaking the decision aloud and thereby making it final, and wondering how I had reached it, if maybe my present emotional state qualified me as temporarily insane.

"We need to gather a few things," I told her.

"Kelvin has a kit, and I stashed some seeds away today. Plus a few other things."

"Were you expecting me to agree to this?" I asked her.

"No, I promise. I had already planned to do it after we talked last night, just in case. I told Kelvin he could take them with him."

I got down from the bench and went to the cab's door; I peered across the floodlit base toward the power module. "There's a few small things I should grab—"

A flash of orange light in the sky interrupted my thoughts. I watched as a streak of plasma lifted up, rising high above the base before exploding with a distant rumble. Tarsi stood and joined me by the glass, both of us peering up at the ball of fire overhead. A moment later, the whistling began, followed by the thudding impacts of bombfruit.

Not as many fell, however, as during the tremors. Not nearly as many. We stood together, our arms around each other as we listened to the odd impact here and there.

"So few," Tarsi said.

"The trees are big," I told her, "but how many of those can they produce? And how fast?"

She leaned her head against my shoulder as the canopy burned overhead. The flames from the incendiary missile spread out in a wide circle of destruction as golden embers rained down, fading to ash long before they reached us, very much how I imagined a meteor shower might look.

"We need to get out of here," Tarsi said sadly.

I couldn't help but agree.

14

CLEARING

KELVIN RETURNED LATE, THE HOUR TECHNICALLY qualifying it as early the next day. He smelled of cordite and smoke and seemed exhausted. When Tarsi broke the news that we were coming with him, his spirits buoyed immediately. He clasped me on the shoulder and tried to express his relief in a series of mumbling and manic half-starts.

Once he calmed down, we sat together on the bench seat and went through his stash of survival gear. He had stopped and picked up Tarsi's seeds and a few other things as well. The only thing I had to offer was a battered flashlight I used when I needed to see around the power module during outages. I added it to a small pack of my own as Kelvin distributed the items between us — the act of sharing our things somehow sealing our resolve to stick together.

Overall, the gear we were meant to survive on was far less than any of us wished we could bring, but if we took any more, our guilt would get the better of us. We figured no one we left behind could fault us for taking so little.

The plan was to leave as soon as the floodlights went off, but after an hour of nervous fidgeting, they remained brightly lit, even though they were usually doused after the day's last shift.

"What are they doing?" Kelvin asked, looking out through a circle he'd swiped in the fogged glass.

"Maybe they're worried about us," I said.

"How would anybody suspect the three of us?" Tarsi asked.

"Not us specifically. I mean everybody. Hickson's gotta know what's going on, what everyone's thinking after Mica and Peter bolted."

Kelvin grunted. "Pretty soon they'll need one enforcer for every worker. Love to see the timetables once that happens."

"We should've left last night," Tarsi said. "And why wouldn't Peter have said something to me about him going? I mean, we were close enough that I'd expect a goodbye or some kind of gesture—not that I think he should've asked us to join."

"Same reason we haven't told anybody," I explained.

Tarsi bit her lip and raised her eyebrows. "I suppose you're right," she finally said.

"So what's the plan?" Kelvin asked, turning from the window. "I say we go anyway. I don't see anyone standing guard. Hell, who in the camp wouldn't pass out if they were asked to take a shift tonight?"

I made my own view port in the misted glass, my hand squealing as it circled. I peered out, then turned to the others. "I say we sneak out of the cab and wait on the landing for a few minutes, see if we spot anybody. Nobody can get onto us just for being up at this hour."

"Good plan," Kelvin said. "And when we move, let's head back past the server module. It's the fastest path to darkness. Once we're out of the light, we can swing around and go through the fence where Mica and Peter escaped."

We each nodded. I tried to set my face and seem as calm as the other two.

Part of me wondered if they were doing the same thing.

After what seemed an eternity on the tractor's landing without a sound—not even a single bombfruit dropping—I led the way down the metal ladder.

As soon as my feet hit the ground, I ducked under the body of the enormous earthmover and hid in the shadow of one of its massive tires. Tarsi came down after, quiet as a sigh, and moved beside me, her hand clutching my arm. Kelvin dropped the last two steps and bent his knees with the fall, landing like a primitive animal poised to strike. As the three of us padded barefoot toward the server module, I admired the lithe movements of the other two and figured of the three of us, I would be the one most likely to get us caught.

The first several hundred feet were the worst. With our surrounds wide open and brightly lit, I felt like our own shadows were trying to turn us in. As we ran away from the low spotlights, the black betrayers grew from our feet, reaching out toward distant modules, threatening to dash up walls and cut across windows. Kelvin waved his hand at us, and we ducked and ran in a crouch, trying to minimize our exposure.

When we reached the server module, I felt like the ordeal must be over. Beyond lay relative darkness. We could cross to what was left of the fuel depot, circle around to the neglected farms, and then work our way past the dump where the debris from our birthday fires had been shoved. We rested on the back side of the module, catching our breaths and making sure our packs were still on our backs and not leaking survival gear.

With my head against the building's exterior, I could hear the machines inside thinking. The servers clicked and whirred, the entire building humming with activity. Kelvin whispered our route one more time, but I didn't hear him. I became lost in the sounds of the servers, the popping of the belts on the recording drives and the buzzing of the fans. It sounded like a machine pulsing and breathing.

Kelvin nodded, seeing if we were ready. He pushed off the wall and began padding his way toward the fuel depot. Tarsi followed, with me right behind.

We were only a dozen feet or so from the module when the Klaxons sounded. The noise was so loud and unexpected, I nearly fell to the ground in paralytic fright. Tarsi and I both stopped and looked back toward the server module, as if unsure which way to run. Kelvin hissed at us both, and my brain — completely undecided — was won over by the urgency in his voice.

We ran. I swung the pack around to my stomach so I could keep it from swinging wildly and concentrated on pumping my legs. Twice, I looked back over my shoulder but could see no sign of pursuit. I followed Tarsi into the blackness of the scavenged fuel depot, only one of its bunkers remaining to hide us. Kelvin grabbed us before we flew past and pulled us close to the lonely cylinder of gold.

"Same route?" Kelvin asked. "Or do we make a new cut?"

The Klaxon was so loud, we had to do more than whisper to be heard. It felt bizarre to consider cutting through a fence meant to protect us and to have our efforts loudly betrayed by a horn meant to warn us of danger.

Tarsi voted we stick to the original route. We had brought some tools for the job, but none of us were quite comfortable with our backup plan of cutting through the fence ourselves.

Kelvin took another look back at the collection of modules and cursed. Tarsi and I looked as well and saw figures moving about, their shadows reaching out dozens of feet across the lit ground.

"They're just being woken up by the horn," Tarsi said.

She was right. The people were milling about as if confused, not running or acting organized. Still, a sense of urgency welled up inside me that threatened to turn into a full panic.

"Let's go," Kelvin said. He pushed off in the direction of the farms. Tarsi and I ran after him, and I began to wonder who had spotted us and sounded the alarm. And why hadn't they yelled for us to stop, or fired a warning shot?

We were halfway to the farms when I figured it out — or at least thought I had. Oliver would have seen it as a sign from the gods, as a bright streak of light fell from the heavens, exploding in a shower of sparks. It was a burning limb from the canopy, more falling debris from the earlier missile firing. I slowed my pace and looked up at the small ring of fire above me. Inside the orange circle of embers loomed a crisp hole of darkest night peppered with bright, winking stars.

And satellites, I thought.

Then it hit me — the timing of the canopy-clearing after someone had escaped. I gazed up at the glimmering pinpricks and continued to jog forward, slamming into Tarsi, who had come to a stop to search the exposed heavens, looking for more falling debris.

"So beautiful," she said.

I pulled her along as I searched the darkness ahead for Kelvin.

Tarsi stumbled, clutching at my shirt. "I can't stop looking at it," she said.

"Yeah," I huffed, trying to catch my breath. "The problem is — I think it's looking *back*."

15

OUTSIDE

AS WE CROSSED OVER THE FALLOW FIELDS AND APproached the dump, the Klaxon fell silent. The end of its blaring brought little relief, however. Our hunters could now be heard shouting throughout the base as they organized our capture. I glanced in their direction as I ran, expecting shots to be fired. The work lights went out, and for a moment I wondered if the tactic would make us easier to spot. But then, over the shouts and barked orders, I heard the hum of the electrified perimeter become louder. All the precious juice had been routed to the fence—more betrayal from the very things meant to protect us.

And more to come, as I heard the tractors roar to life and realized our own sleep-home was going to be used to hunt us down.

The three of us paused by the dump to catch our breath. Tarsi clung to me—I could feel her shaking. All of us had physically deteriorated since leaving the vats, slowly wasting away on poor sleep and a poorer diet. Even if we somehow escaped capture, we had begun our sojourn by burning precious calories before we even got beyond the fence and started eking out some sort of life on our own.

One of the tractors revved angrily. The lights from its cab moved out past the modules and toward the break in the fence.

"We need to hurry," Tarsi said, her breathing labored.

The three of us ran for the spot where Mica and Peter had gone through. To the side, I could see the two tractors rumbling across the clearing, one of them clearly heading to the old break. Kelvin increased his lead, disappearing into the darkness as we neared the inner ditch, the berm beyond, and the tall and buzzing fence.

Tarsi and I shuffled down through the steep rut and scrambled up the berm. Kelvin cursed and fumbled in his pack for something. The fence hummed furiously above us; I crawled up even with Kelvin to see what was taking him so long.

The fence had been patched.

Solid replacement bars were welded across the breach. None of us had heard plans made for the repair that day, nor had anything been put on the timetables for the work. We had brought along insulated cutters and wire in case we needed to make our own hole, but there seemed little time with the search party already hunting us. Looking back toward base, I saw the tractor halfway to the fence already, lumbering along with a menacing roar.

"What do we do?" Tarsi asked.

I started to suggest we follow the ditch, sneak back into camp, blend in with the search party, and pretend we were never attempting to flee. Then, figures materialized out of the darkness, coming for us along the ditch. And I realized it was too late.

"Porter? Tarsi?" Jorge scampered up the berm toward us—the fear in his eyes marking him as a fellow escapee, not a warden on the prowl. Several other shapes materialized in the ditch, more people converging on yesterday's exit.

"Make the cuts!" I yelled back to Kelvin, who had already begun doing just that. I ran down the berm and helped several others up, watching the tractor and people on foot make their way toward us. Cones of light splayed out from a few of the walkers as they scanned the ground with flashlights.

The Klaxon went off again, hopefully a sign Kelvin had made the first cut, not bothering with the wires. Three other people scampered up past me. I looked back and saw a pathetic, trembling crowd huddled by the fence, waiting for a way out. But the tractor and the men were going to get to us before we made it through. The machine's headlights illuminated the ground just a hundred feet from us, but that distance was steadily decreasing.

My feet made my next decision for me. They led me out of the ditch and straight toward the headlights—my resolve laboring to catch up. When it did, I found myself running to meet the tractor and the walking, searching silhouettes. Over the buzzing of the fence and the revving of the engine, I heard Tarsi yell out for me, but even that didn't shake me to my senses.

As soon as I hit the edge of the tractor's lights, a set of shouts rang out from ahead, our pursuers barking with excitement at having made contact.

I turned to the side and ran parallel to the fence, hoping to draw the light away.

I drew gunfire instead.

A loud pop shot out over the hum of the tractor, and something whistled through the air above my head, another reversal of the bomb-fruit sounds.

Again. Bang and whistle.

I ducked my head reflexively and churned my legs. After the next pop, a fountain of dirt erupted ahead of me. I had to force myself to not slow down, keeping in mind a moving target would be harder to hit. When I neared the edge of the tractor's cone of light—almost back into darkness—I heard more shouting. Directions were yelled. The light turned, keeping me in its sight, taking us both away from the hole in the fence.

The pops started coming in groups, the buzzing and plumes of dirt surrounding me. I had pressed my luck too far. I veered back toward the perimeter, sprinting hard for the ditch as the tractor's headlamps illuminated the high fence beyond. Diving for the edge, I tumbled inside, my small pack of supplies flying loose and spilling across the dirt. Like a fool, I clutched for a few of the precious items. I felt my flashlight rolling through the dirt and grabbed it. I groped for other items, then the thumps of running feet jarred me back to the danger behind.

Keeping my head low, I doubled back toward the hole in the fence, wondering if I'd given Kelvin half the time he needed. I had almost reached the edge of the tractor's lights when I heard grunts behind me—enforcers spilling into the ditch. Another pop, and the berm erupted with a shower of soil. I had no idea if I was getting lucky, or if they just had horrid aim. I had no idea how difficult it was to operate a handgun while on the move.

With no need to hide any longer, I kept my head up so I could run faster, and I saw over the lip of the ditch that the first tractor was backing up and making a slow turn to follow. The second machine bore down on the breach in the fence. The pursuit was converging on the most logical point of escape—the same bad idea that had brought us all together that night.

After another flurry of pops sounded from behind, I felt something pinch my thigh. I hobbled for a few steps, thinking I'd been shot, but the pain wasn't nearly as bad as I thought it would be. Ahead of me, the dark shapes of my fellow escapees came into view, and then the floodlights of the second tractor lit them up like what I imagined raw unfiltered daylight to be like.

More shots, followed by the zing of metal on metal. I noticed the group had grown smaller than when I'd left them and hoped that meant the hole was open. Running as fast as I could, my lungs burning from the effort, I glanced back at the enforcers and saw they weren't moving much faster. They were just as winded as me.

Up the berm I went, scrambling for the hole as the cluster of bodies at the top seemed to have been whittled down to just a few. I pushed up behind someone, urging them forward as dirt exploded around us. Another shot ricocheted off the fence above us with a loud zing. The legs ahead of me flew out of sight and I fell forward, pressing myself flat against the dirt, throwing my arms through the hole. All around me was the loud buzzing of a quick death. One touch and my body would be cooked, smoking and burning like the falling heads of my nightmares, like all my vat-mates who hadn't made it —

Several pairs of hands grasped me from outside. I couldn't even kick my legs to help; they just yanked me through, all of us tumbling down the other side of the berm, where we rolled through the dirt, panting and wheezing.

Before we could take stock or enjoy the weak thrill of freedom, we found ourselves running again, wary of the chance of pursuit from behind, overcome with the odd sensation of a fenceless horizon as we stumbled into darkness and the perilous unknown.

PART II

INTO THE UNKNOWN

16

OLD FRIENDS

MORNING CAME, ITS FEEBLE RAYS SLANTING through the dense canopy overhead and winding around trees that rose up in great cliffs of wood. Our group lay together in a tight cluster, our heads on each other. Exhaustion had overtaken a few of us just an hour into our hike through the blackness. Despite protestations, I had been unwilling to hazard the light for fear of being spotted. Of the three flashlights that had been brought between all the escapees, mine was the only one that had survived our mad push through the fence.

Sitting up, I noticed a few others had awoken before me. Kelvin, Vincent, and Britny—the last a girl I hardly knew—sat together a dozen paces away, whispering and allowing the rest of us to enjoy our sleep. I disentangled myself from Tarsi and tried to stand, only to feel a stabbing pain in the back of my thigh. Hobbling away from the other sleepers, I moved halfway to Kelvin before collapsing.

"Are you okay?" he whispered, coming to my side.

"I think I got shot last night," I told him. "Forgot all about it. Didn't hurt much till now."

"Roll over," he said, trying to keep his voice low, his worry threatening to wake the others.

I lay face-down in the mossy ground cover and saw Vincent and Britny casting me confused looks. I waved—partly from embarrassment—as Kelvin pulled my trousers down to inspect the wound. They both waved back, and something in the normalcy of the gesture amused me. We were failed planetary colonists on the run from our own people, out in the middle of an unexplored planet that supposedly teetered between viability and abort. And there we were, waving at one another with sheepish grins, taking stock of who had made the break, who had been fed up with their lives enough to chance throwing them away.

"Ow," I hissed, as Kelvin found my wound and probed it with his hand. He brought something up in front of my face.

"A shard of rock," he said, holding the bloody stone dart up for me to see. "Barely a scratch."

I rolled over and worked my pants back into place. Kelvin helped me up, and it felt like a lot more than a scratch on the back of my leg. I limped over to the others, who shifted in place to include me.

"Doesn't feel like a scratch," I told Kelvin, enjoying the sensation of being half carried and half escorted by him.

"There might be a little bruising as well," he admitted. "But trust me, your little legs will be fine."

I rolled my eyes.

"Hello, Porter," Vincent said as I joined them on the ground.

I smiled and greeted them both. "So, the disenfranchised among us make themselves known," I said.

"Yeah, and I'm sure there'll be more," Britny said, frowning.

I looked to Kelvin. "Speaking of which, we need to find Mica and Peter. I can't stand the thought of them out here alone." I looked over my shoulder. "There's what? Nearly ten of us?"

"Maybe this will be enough to change the way things are running around base," Vincent said. "This many people gone—using another half dozen for enforcement—the timetables are gonna go to shit."

"Chances are it'll just make things at camp worse for the rest," I said.

"How?" Britny asked.

"A dozen ways. They could tighten the perimeter now that the farms have been abandoned and the fuel depot has been picked apart. There's enough fencing there for two smaller nested circuits if they wanted to do that. Or they could pack everyone into a few modules every night and lock them up. And if I can think of these things, I'm sure Hickson can come up with something even worse."

"I don't know that it's all Hickson," Vincent said. "I think he's just Colony's muscle."

Kelvin shook his head. "No way," he said. "Everything went south when Stevens died."

"And I'm not convinced Hickson killed Stevens," Vincent told him.

"We need to start worrying about ourselves," Britny said. "The next few weeks are gonna make the last few seem like a night in the vats."

"And Colony was predicting rain for tonight. I heard it from Myra."

Someone squeezed my shoulder from behind. I turned as Tarsi sat down beside me. She leaned her head against my shoulder, and I glanced up in time to see the pained expression on Kelvin's face, which he quickly wiped away.

"How did you sleep?" I asked her.

"Bad dreams, but otherwise . . . okay. How are you?"

"He's got a boo-boo on his girly little leg," Kelvin said, pointing and smiling.

"Are you hurt?"

I shrugged. "It's nothing."

Kelvin smiled. "That's not what you said a minute ago."

I glared at him. His smile broadened, but he raised his hands in mock surrender.

Britny stood and rested her hands on her hips. "When you boys are done fooling around, we need to make some decisions. How far do we go before we start digging in? Everybody seems to have grabbed a thing or two before they left, so how are we dividing these things up? Or *are* we?"

Tarsi, Kelvin, and I looked at one another. We hadn't planned on

any of that. The three of us were family, so there was no question of
what belonged to whom. As much as we needed and supported everyone else, the idea of submitting to another collective when the goal of
that *new* group might one day turn out to be as sensible as building
rockets—it didn't sit well with me. I could see similar worries on the
faces of my friends.

"We *are* in this together, aren't we?" Britny asked.

We sat silent for a moment.

Several of us nodded slightly, as we looked to one another. I turned
at the sound of people moving behind me and saw some of the sleepers stirring and stretching, pointing up to the new patch of open sky
overhead created by last night's missile.

"This is going to get complicated awfully quick," I grumbled.

"No, it's not," Jorge said behind us. "Let me make it real simple. I
brought a gun." I turned and saw him reaching behind his back. He
pulled his hand out and pointed two fingers at us, then started laughing.

Eventually, the rest of us joined in.

Though I, for one, never saw the humor in it.

An easy and temporary consensus formed once everyone was up and
had gathered their things together. We decided we would walk toward
the nearest tree-things, just to make sure that they really were just ex-
traterrestrial plant life. Several of us were curious to see one up close
after having lived within sight of them for weeks. They were so unlike
the trees from our training programs that they seemed utterly alien to
us, even though we'd never truly known anything else.

From the colony, they had appeared continuous, a jagged cliff of
rising bark that encircled us completely. The width of each trunk was
easily as big around as the perimeter of our entire base. Between the
closest trees you could see darker trunks looming in the shadowy distance. They overlapped in a way that blocked out all else, creating the
appearance of something solid and impenetrable. As we neared them,

they appeared even broader and flatter, their curvature removed by our proximity.

We set off toward the nearest one, figuring that would have been Mica and Peter's plan too. We could make shelter along the wall of wood, affixing our various scraps of canvas to stay out of the rain, and maybe use our machetes to remove building material from the trunk.

Even with the pain in my hamstring, the walk was a pleasant one. The previous night, we had discovered that the surface of our planet wasn't all packed dirt and mud, which was all we'd ever seen inside our fenced-in colony. Everything Colony prepared for us, out to a hundred yards or more, had been beaten down by constantly roaming tractors and dozers.

Now that we were finally moving past Colony's reach, we could see what the ground of our home normally looked like: mostly moss. A half-dozen varieties covered the ground beneath the canopy. Some were soft, others stiff, but all were better than the hard soil that had calloused our feet over the past weeks. We soon learned the brown mosses and the really dark green ones were the most abrasive, so our line swayed to and fro as we picked out the most luxuriant paths.

We also quickly discovered the bombfruit hadn't evolved to explode on impact. Out beyond the perimeter, they studded the ground like stones—half-buried, the pointy ends embedded in the moss. They looked like seeds pushed partway into the ground by a giant's thumb. None of them seemed to be sprouting anything, however, and the dearth of natural sunlight didn't seem to bode well for their chances of growing into more trees.

Kelvin, with his training as a farmer, was the nearest we had to a botanist in the group. He seemed fascinated by the seeds. The rest of us were just glad to know we would starve to death no more rapidly out here than we would have inside the camp.

The only other curiosity we came across on our way to the tree was an odd geological formation: a hole, almost perfectly round, big enough to swallow a tractor whole, that gaped in the middle of the moss. Our path nearly took us right into it, causing us to stop and peer inside. The shaft seemed to go straight down, far deeper than my flashlight could penetrate. Karl, an electrician who had been shuffled between construction and payload duty a few times, took a bombfruit and threw it into the center. We all stood quietly until we heard a distant clatter, then marveled at what the depth of the thing must be.

We left the strange hole behind and resolved to no longer run through the night like madmen. Just in case. Tarsi hammered the point home when she spotted another of the holes in the distance. Nobody spoke of the chances that Mica and Peter wouldn't be found, but I couldn't have been the only one thinking it.

It took half the day before we reached the trunk, the thing seeming to slide away from us one step for every two we took. The base of it was even more massive than we had imagined. As we marveled at it, Kelvin noted that he had overheard the canopy crew adjusting their missile the other night for a height of two thousand feet. It was hard to believe a living thing could grow to such proportions, but the evidence loomed before us.

We stopped several hundred feet away and made lunch out of raw bombfruit with a pinch of spice someone had brought along. Objectively, it was less palatable than the paste we normally ate, but we all agreed the novelty of the mixture made it somehow more enjoyable. Or perhaps it was just that the food and the time spent consuming it were *ours*.

Several people wondered aloud what the rest of the camp was doing right then, besides hating our guts. Those with intimate knowledge of the timetables told us precisely what each group would be doing and even what some of us were supposed to be up to. I sat facing the distant camp, the tops of the modules barely visible above the rise of the berm. A spot of raw sunlight beamed down from the new hole in the canopy overhead, glimmering off the things we could no longer use. It all looked so small. So impossible. How was such a speck of humanity expected to tame an entire planet? And what did that make our little group? A mote ejected from the speck?

Halfway through the meal, rapid popping noises sounded in the direction of the colony. Even if the berm and fence weren't there, we were too far away to see individual people moving around camp, leaving us to speculate.

"The propellant?"

"Sabotage," Jorge said, almost with a hint of wishing.

"It's a warning."

A twinge in the back of my leg—a sudden jolt of pain—gave me the answer:

"Target practice," I said.

We fell silent and the popping sounds did as well. We looked around at one another as the noise started back up a minute later. Those who had obsessed with timetables for two weeks murmured their disgust at the labor hours needed to replenish all those rounds of ammo.

Overall, the meal could not have been more bizarre. It was, in many ways, even stranger than the first one we'd had the morning after our birth. That one had been so consumed with depression and despair that no other emotion could gain purchase. This one had a tinge of accidental camaraderie, as fully three separate groups had made our break on the same night—all following in Mica's and Peter's footsteps. While we ate, Kelvin admitted that the three of us had dreamed of escaping a day earlier. Four of the others, including Vincent and Britny, had even discussed the idea before the enforcers formed up.

As a half-trained psychologist, I was fascinated by how quickly the group gelled. Many of my fears concerning shared resources faded as I spoke and joked with each person. Names and faces I knew in passing were now a part of my tribe, and over the course of a single morning, I went from feeling wary of their presence to being willing to risk myself for them. And not just like the night before, where my primary concern had been for Kelvin and Tarsi, but really put myself in danger for any one of them. Whatever the cause of this magical transformation, I had not yet come to it in my studies of human behavior.

After we ate as much of the foul-tasting fruit as we could and passed around our several rations of water, we rose as a group and approached the tree. The organism seemed to offer a hello—or possibly a warning—as a single bombfruit whistled out of the canopy and buried itself with a thud inside a nearby patch of light green moss. We laughed at the timing and stepped around the embedded fruit as if it still contained some animating force. We spread out to explore the mountainous plant.

"It's *soft*," Samson said.

He was one of the two boys who had brought machetes. I saw him rubbing the blade against a jagged edge of bark, peeling a piece back with ease.

The skin might be soft, but the shape of the tree was rough, far more than it had appeared from a distance. The bark was so jagged and the spacing of the outcrops so regular, you could step inside the wide crevasses and find yourself surrounded on three sides by cool, brown walls of tree. It reminded me of a mechanical gear if seen top-down, like evenly spaced cogs standing out from a round, recessed base.

Several of us stepped between the cogs into what felt like roofless caves. I went all the way inside one of the creases and looked up, mesmerized by the way the bark wiggled its way up into the canopy. It no longer looked like a cave but more like a square, vertical ditch running all the way up the surface of the tree, the edges seeming to converge in the distance.

I put my back against one of the walls jutting out from the center and tried to place my hands against the opposite side, wondering if a taller person could shimmy their way up to the branches and leaves overhead. It would take monumental endurance.

"Give me fruuuiiiiit," someone howled, and we all laughed at the way the vertical canyon toyed with their voice. I popped out of my indentation and imagined us carving a little village right out of the trunk, all of our individual caves interconnected. We could dig up some mosses and plant our Terran seeds in the soil, see if they would grow in the filtered sunlight. The tarps we could save for gathering and storing water. I stepped back and looked up the tree, imagining how we could make it work.

Tarsi came up behind me and wrapped her arms around my stomach. I turned into her embrace and gave her a joyous squeeze. To our side, I saw Kelvin step away from the tree and glance over at us, that expression from earlier on his face. I waved him over and he grudgingly joined in our little group hug.

"I'm gonna miss our tractor," he said.

"Even on floor night?" Tarsi asked.

"Even then."

"I wish Oliver was here," I told the others, breaking out of the hug and looking back in the direction of base.

"Yeah," Kelvin said. "I wonder what he—"

"Hey! Check this out!" Vincent backed away from the tree and pointed. He had wandered fifty feet or so farther down the trunk. We all ran over to see what he'd found.

"Did you carve that?" Samson asked, pointing his machete at one of the outcroppings of bark.

"With what?" Vincent said, shrugging his shoulders and lifting his empty hands.

I pushed past the people up front to see. Leila stood right next to the tree, rubbing her hands over it.

It was an arrow. Carved into the trunk.

Pointing up.

17

INCLINATIONS

"NONE OF YOU CARVED THIS?" LEILA ASKED.

"How are we supposed to go up?" someone said.

"Why should we?" Kelvin asked. "I don't want to be up there. If it was Mica or Peter who made this, let them come down here and join us."

"I don't like being on this side of the tree," Vincent said. "If we're really looking to survive for the long term, setting up camp next to the people we abandoned might not be the best plan."

"I agree," Britny said. "We should make our way around one of these guys and set up camp on the other side. Maybe move even farther as we explore. For all we know, there's open fields on the other side of this thing."

"No way," Jorge said. "Colony wouldn't have cut its way through the canopy and set up here if there was open space like that nearby. I'd be surprised if there was a clearing this big anywhere else in the temperate zone. It would've picked the best spot. That's like its primary job."

"What were you trained for?" I asked Jorge.

"I'm a miner, but that doesn't make me any less smart than you."

"Whoa," I said, holding up my hands. "Just curious."

He shook his head and looked away, and I resolved to step lightly around him from then on.

"Guys, I found the way up."

We turned and looked farther down the trunk where Mindy stood, her hand on an outcropping of bark several paces away. The crowd shifted again, curiosity driving us along.

"Holy shit," one of the guys said, looking up the trunk of the tree.

It was a spiral tunnel, rising up and off to the side, farther around the base. The angle wasn't too steep, and the carved indentation ran behind the gear-like outcroppings, exposing the inclined plane to air before weaving behind the next outcropping, and so on. Kelvin stepped between two of the juts and ran his hand along the exposed core of the tree.

"Something created that," Samson said.

"No shit."

"I mean, like, chewed that out."

"He's right," Kelvin said. He ducked his head into the cylinder of missing wood and looked up the incline. "I wonder how far it goes?"

"You're not thinking about exploring it, are you?"

"Maybe we should," Vincent said.

"I say forget about it," Mindy said.

"What about the arrow?"

"Probably Mica and Peter throwing off pursuit."

"Yeah, why would they think other people would come out and join them?" Mindy asked. "They could be trying to get Hickson killed as much as helping us find them."

"She has a good point."

"It worms back down that way," Kelvin said, looking through the shaft in the direction we'd come. "I think it comes out behind the arrow."

Vincent ran down and stepped between the two outcroppings back at the carving. "It does," he said. "I still think we should explore it."

Tarsi turned to Mindy. "It must be biological," she said. "The difference in us, I mean. The boys want to go up it, and the girls want to circle around and set up camp."

I didn't say anything, wondering what it meant that I agreed with the girls on that score. Perhaps my training had me more attuned to risk.

"Maybe there's all kinds of passageways dug through the trees," we heard Vincent say, his voice muffled. He popped his head out where Kelvin stood, having walked up through the tunnel from where the arrow was. "Maybe there's all kinds of cool caves to live in, and we could save the digging."

"Hey, genius, whatever ate those holes are probably still around. You think they'll let us just move in with them?"

"Maybe they taste good," someone said, which made us all fall silent. I watched the thought settle throughout the group, lips literally being licked.

"Meat," one of the boys said.

"You've never had meat in your life," Leila pointed out.

"Yeah, but I know it's good," Jorge said. "It's *primal.*"

"*You're* primal," Britny said, which got more than a few of us laughing.

"I say we vote," Kelvin said, scanning the crowd.

"No fair," said Tarsi. "There's six of you and only four of us."

"What if we do *both?*" I asked, hoping to prevent my exposure as a wimp or having to fake some machismo I didn't feel. "Why don't some of us set up camp, get a fire going, rig up some cover in case of rain. Meanwhile, a scouting party can go partway up the tree, look around a little, maybe find Mica and Peter if they're up there."

"Sounds good to me," Vincent said. I looked up to follow his voice and saw his hand reaching out between two of the outcroppings farther along.

"I don't like the idea of splitting up," Tarsi said, looking directly at me.

"I'll stay here and help with camp," I said, shrugging as if I'd just as well scale a tree but didn't mind staying for her benefit.

She smiled. I looked to the tree and saw Kelvin glowering at us before he was able to store the emotion away again.

"You guys can take the flashlight," I told him. "Just in case it gets dark before you get all the way back down."

He nodded and forced a smile. I realized how badly I needed to talk to him and wondered when I would ever get the time.

Before the boys set off, we all dumped our packs and arranged our meager supplies across the moss. More than half the water went to the climbers. We kept the tarps, most of the rope, one of the machetes, and all the domestic gear. They took the small amount of medical supplies and packed several bombfruit in their sacks. We agreed they would climb only until nightfall, then descend with the flashlight, but Vincent and Kelvin argued they could set up camp within the incline, behind one of the outcroppings, and descend the next day.

The rest of us relented once the other boys got excited about the idea. We also resolved that if they found anything important or discovered passageways through the interior, they would yell down or send a messenger back before they explored any further.

We exchanged hugs and wished each other luck. I felt awkward and conspicuous as the only male not joining the climbers, but as soon as they disappeared, the five of us who stayed behind immediately set to work. We agreed that the tunnel provided the best place for sleep, so we concentrated on clearing and creating a fire pit, carving burnable wood from one of the outcroppings, and gathering bombfruit.

Mindy and Tarsi had worked in supply together and knew how to split the occasional intact fruit in half, both sides of which created functional bowls. They gathered the soft gold seeds from the interior, which Britny and I took for creating utensils. We picked one of the large stones sticking out of the moss and dug up a few smaller ones.

Using one to beat against the other, we turned the seeds into functional shapes for spooning and mixing.

We dug the fire pit out by hand and stone, then lined it with the latter. Fiber from the inside of the bombfruit was laid out to dry, and several of us took turns with the machete to perform the arduous task of carving out strips of firewood from the trunk. We quickly learned that the best method entailed holding the handle with one hand and gripping the dull side of the blade with a handful of moss in the other. Then the machete could be pulled down the outcropping, peeling back a layer of wood with each pass. It proved laborious work, but we all tried to shoulder our fair share of it. We also agreed that the fire wasn't to be wasted. We would light it when it got dark and enjoy its warmth before going to sleep.

The afternoon went by quickly, thanks to the work. We passed the time and toil by chatting and getting to know one another better. I found myself talking pre-birthday stuff for the first time, and several others did as well. So much of our lives had been spent in a virtual world that no one else knew anything about. The professional training we took for granted—that which the colony had ended up with little use for—finally came out.

Sadly, not much of what our small group had been taught seemed useful for starting an agrarian culture on a remote planet, but all of it fascinated the others and helped explain quite a bit of our personality differences and our philosophies on life. Teachers just don't see the world the same way tailors do, and vice versa.

As the sun set and the fire was finally lit, we reclined in the moss, our heads on each other's bellies in a tangle of repose. It reminded me of the manner in which we'd passed out the night before. As we lay, touching, we swapped guesses on what the boys were encountering. We also talked about who —if such a thing were possible—we wished we could teleport out of the camp to join us. We even debated what the current timetable for the rocket must look like, the habit of our shared project not leaving us nearly as easily as we'd left it.

That evening seemed simple enough. A small group of us spent it stretched out on the moss, just listening to each other's voices and tossing out our own. And yet, of all my time on our unnamed planet thus far, it was one of the best, most normal nights of my entire waking life.

I wish there could've been more of them.

18

MEAT

WHAT BEGAN AS A PLEASANT EVENING SOON TURNED into a miserable night's sleep. We tried to make ourselves comfortable in the chewed-out tunnel, but it proved nearly impossible. We had to lie directly on the rough wood—the wet canvas became too slick, causing us to slide toward our feet as we tried to drift off. Eventually, we moved back to the soft moss by the fire, enjoying the warmth from the glowing embers.

But then it started raining. Heavy, like the day we were born. We returned to the tree and spent the rest of the night trying to get comfortable without ever truly succeeding. There was a lot of talk about how the boys must be faring and how it made no sense to be out exploring the unknown when we should be working to sustain ourselves for the future.

Despite the discomfort and a night of tossing, turning, whispering, and complaining, I found myself waking up the next morning, the light of day making the leftover rain sparkle in the moss. The waking meant I must have slept. And the rain meant we had fresh water to go with our breakfast.

I exited the tunnel and stretched my aching back. Britny was already up and filling water pouches from the collection tarps we'd left out, their centers in shallow depressions we'd dug by hand, the edges raised with piles of moss.

"Morning," I said, grabbing my canvas thermos with its stitched and glued edges and filling it up with a single scoop.

"Did you sleep?" Britny asked.

"For the last hour or so. You?"

She shook her head. I turned around and looked up the wall of corrugated bark, wondering how far the boys had gone up and if they were already on their way back down.

"Did you hear the horn go off last night?" Britny asked.

"The Klaxon? From the base?"

She nodded. "Just before sunup. Only sounded for fifteen minutes or so."

"I must've been asleep," I said. I took a sip of the water and held it in my mouth while I allowed it to be absorbed. Swallowing what remained, I wiped my mouth with my sleeve and looked toward the distant and fuzzy line of black, the tall perimeter fence barely discernible. "Should we sneak closer and investigate?"

Britny shrugged. "Been wondering the same thing." She pouted her lower lip and wrinkled her forehead. With her dark skin and jet-black hair, it made her look lovely and menacing at the same time. I found myself liking her even though I didn't know her as well as some of the others.

After a moment of seemingly intense concentration, she shook her head and reached for another water pouch to fill.

"What?" I asked.

"Hmm?"

"What were you thinking just now?"

"Oh, just whether or not we should go back. See if someone else left. Then I was wondering why someone would make their break early in the morning. And would they find us here? Will Hickson send people out to look for us? Then I . . ."

I moved to the other side of the collection tarp and took the water sack from her, folding the flap over and tying off the neck. "You what?" I asked.

"I wonder if it was wrong to leave," she said. "If maybe I was being impulsive. Maybe I just needed a day off, and then I would've been fine. It— I know it sounds weird, but I did enjoy the work at times. And I wanted to see the rocket go up, you know? I just didn't want to live in fear, and now I wonder if we'll be living in a different kind of fear. What will it be like if we do set up something permanent, and then the people at the base manage to do well? How long before there's some sort of conflict?"

I put my arm around her. We remained on our knees in front of the collection tarp, her head leaning to the side and resting on my shoulder.

"When you have doubts, remember the things that made you want to flee," I told her. "That's what I do. There were good times, but they were only good because everything to either side was absolute shit."

Britny laughed and wiped at her cheeks. "You're right," she said. "Maybe we need some really bad stuff to happen out here so we can appreciate the less crappy stuff."

"Don't jinx us," I said, looking over the tarp and back at the tree. Through a gap in the bark, I could see a few sleeping forms stirring. And Tarsi—I could see her sitting up—she was looking out at the two of us and smiling.

Of all the brutal days endured thus far on our strange planet—the cleanup following our birth, the eighteen-hour work shifts for the rocket project, the restless nights of exhaustion—none was ever so long as that day of waiting for the boys to return. And waiting. And doing nothing.

Several times, we lamented the fact that a scouting party, just two or three of us, could have gone to the breach in the fence and returned already, determining the reason for the horn sounding. After lunch

—during which there was another round of distant target practice—
the concern was raised that the boys wouldn't be back before nightfall. By dinner, it was all we spoke of. As it grew dark, we stretched out
by the fire, lying across the sumptuous moss, resting on one another,
and sleeping as poorly as we had the night before, but for different
reasons.

Tarsi and I lay with our heads together—hers on my arm—as we
tried to convince one another Kelvin was okay. Most of the night was
like that, whispers and fidgeting and people sneaking off to pee. Even
the faint glimmer of stars through the new clearing in the distance did
nothing to soothe my mind. Once again, I feared I would never sleep,
only to wake up to another missed dawn.

Gruff voices and laughter wormed their way into my dreams. I snapped
awake, rousing Tarsi, who had fallen asleep on my stomach. We both
turned toward the sounds. Some small part of me feared it was a group
from base coming to force us to go back, but the voices seemed to be
leaking out of the tree.

Leaning forward, I smoothed Tarsi's hair, kissed her forehead, and
told her I'd be right back.

I ran for the tree. Several of the girls stirred as I left the group, the
voices from the tree becoming clearer. I jumped into the sloping tunnel and hurried up, my feet gripping the rough, exposed wood—the
soreness in my hamstring forgotten.

Because of the slope of the tunnel and the wide tree's nearly non-
existent curvature, I saw their feet and generic pants first, so I couldn't
tell each owner's identity. I thought I heard Kelvin's voice in the crowd
and tried my best to tease his tenor out from the rest as I hurried along.

I came to Vincent first. When he saw me running to greet them,
he smiled and shook his head from side to side as if to chastise me for
all the fun I'd missed. I squeezed past him, patted him on the back
warmly, and came next to Kelvin, who beamed at seeing me.

"What took so long?" I asked. I turned and walked down alongside him; the round tunnel was plenty wide enough as long as we each walked up the curving floor a little.

"We got so close to the top on that first day," Kelvin said. "In the morning we decided to keep heading up instead of going down. Wait till you see what we found."

"Mica and Peter?"

"Not exactly," he said, reaching over and squeezing my shoulder. "They definitely came this way, though."

"So what is it?" I asked.

"The critters that made this." He slapped the tunnel with his hand.

We heard screaming ahead of us as the girls encountered Vincent. Kelvin and I hurried forward, jumping out when the gap in the spiral became low enough off the ground. Tarsi leaped up and hugged Kelvin's neck, her feet swinging away from him as he spun her around. As soon as he let her go, she slapped him on the arm for worrying us, and Kelvin laughed out of habit.

"We need to get a fire going," he said.

I noticed — now that we were out of the tunnel and in the wan light of dawn — that his face had turned bright pink, especially his nose. Behind him, Samson jumped down from the tree, and hugs were exchanged in every permutation possible.

I set to work on the fire, building a nice vertical pyramid of fruit husks and shaved wood. While I flicked the back of the machete against the magnesium block, I listened to snippets of three different conversations at once, each boy trying to answer a half-dozen simultaneous queries.

I heard the word "excruciating" more than once when asked about the hike up. "Glorious" regarding what they'd found. And they wouldn't stop teasing the big surprise that was coming — and why it was taking Jorge and Karl a bit longer.

Once the fire was sparked, I leaned down and blew on it to catch the husk, then closed my little pyramid by leaning a few thin strips of bark across the opening. Tarsi had already made a trip to the base of the tunnel to bring me the firewood we'd stored there in case of rain. I sorted through the pieces and leaned a few smaller ones around the growing flames. I wasn't sure what Kelvin wanted with the fire, seeing that the morning was quite warm already, but they were the ones who had just scaled to the treetops, so the least I could do was chop some more wood.

I cut a few fat logs out of the tree by hacking the top of one outcrop's corner, then the bottom, before finally prying out the loosened piece with the edge of the blade. Kelvin pulled himself away from the chatter around the fire and came over; Tarsi followed along.

"You need help?" he asked.

"Are you kidding? After what you just went through?" I took another swing with the machete, concentrating on doing it well now that I had an audience.

"Coming down was easy," he said. "We were joking around the entire time, pausing to take in the view."

"What was it like?"

"The other night was miserable, with the rain and all. But yesterday was unreal. The clouds blew off, and the entire sky was as blue as the hole we made in the canopy. Only, it was as far as you could see. Just bright blue all around. And you can move around up there, the canopy is so tight on top. And—well, I want you both to see it for yourself."

I laughed and shook my head before taking another swipe at the base of the tree. "I'll take your word for it. I don't think I'd enjoy the hike or the height."

Kelvin stepped up and helped me pry loose a hunk of wood the size of my arm. "Nonsense," he said. "The hike isn't that bad."

"You used the word 'excruciating.'"

"That was because I didn't know it would be worth it at the time. Damn, Porter, just say you'll go."

"Maybe after the harvest," I said, kicking a few splinters on the ground out of my way and readying the machete for another hack.

"The *harvest?* We have a long way to go before we even clear some land and plant some seeds."

"Exactly." I took a swipe at the tree, the blade singing with a poor blow. "What were you saying about Mica and Peter?"

"We found another carving at the top, so they were definitely there. It pointed across the canopy, away from base, but we could see in all directions without any sign of them."

"How far did the canopy spread?" Tarsi asked.

"There's a ridge of mountains west of here. Steep and snowcapped. Our heavy rains must be caused by them."

I set the machete down and tried to recall what Kelvin had taught us about rain clouds—but I couldn't remember. While prying another hunk of wood loose, I saw Samson casually drop two more small logs on the fire and realized I was falling behind.

"West is away from base," I said, thinking out loud. "That's where the arrow was pointing?"

"Yeah, why? Wait—are you thinking that's where Mica and Peter were going? Why would they head to the mountains?"

I shrugged. "Why would they climb the tree?"

A surge of noise erupted from the girls, a cacophony of squeals, shrieks, and outright screams. I turned, expecting to find at least three of them on fire, and nearly fell over at the sight of the creature coming out of the tree next to me.

It looked like a furry snake but was bigger than a man lying on his belly. Three times as big and four times as long. Its body was covered in bristles that waved along its length, seeming to propel it forward. I reached for the machete and backed away, my heart thudding in my chest. Kelvin laughed at me and took a step forward; he grabbed a loop of rope tied around the creature's foremost end.

The hysterics from the girls continued as a second creature came out after the first, its head almost touching the other's rear.

"Come on!" Kelvin yelled at me. He pulled on the rope, steering the first creature away from the tree and across the moss. I ran after him but kept my distance.

"What the hell are those things?" I shouted.

"We call 'em vinnies," Kelvin said. "In honor of Vincent, who nearly jumped to his death when he discovered them. Or, rather, when *they* discovered *him*."

I backed away from the thing as Kelvin swung it my way, bringing its face into view. The stiff hairs ended a foot from the tip, the brown and black follicles leading to a light green head with two large, moist, charcoal eyes. A stick extended out from the thing's back, tied there by loops of rope.

"Their faces are kinda cute," I said.

"They look like giant Earth caterpillars," Kelvin told me. "Nearest thing I know of, anyway."

"I don't know what those look like, so I'll take your word for it. I immediately thought 'snake' when it came out."

Kelvin laughed. "Yeah, I suppose not many people have phobias of caterpillars."

"What's the stick for?" I asked.

"Propulsion. They eat these leaf-like chips from the tree. We hung one ahead of it to get it started down. Must've fallen off."

"I let him eat it once we got to the bottom," Vincent said. He ran up to help Kelvin steer the creature. "Figured he deserved it." I looked back at the tree and saw a third vinnie had exited the tunnel, the nose of the fourth right behind.

"How many did you guys bring down?"

"Seven, if they all stayed together."

"Why?" I asked. "What're we gonna do with them?"

Kelvin and Vincent both looked up at me as they continued to guide the lead vinnie.

"Are you kidding?" Jorge asked, walking up behind me. I turned and saw him slapping his hand with the side of his machete.

"We're gonna eat them."

19

THE SLAUGHTER

JORGE AND KARL LED ONE OF THE VINNIES ASIDE. The remaining six marched in a circle, the lead vinnie having been guided around until his nose met the last one's rump. The entire column writhed, their brown and black thistles waving over and over down the length of each body. I was as hungry as the rest, but for some reason I didn't like the idea of eating something alive. I could find nothing in my training so different from the other colonists to justify my lone revolt, but nobody else seemed to be bothered by the idea.

I tried talking to Kelvin about it, but Jorge and Karl began mocking me, and I could see confusion on Kelvin's face as well. After being called a "sissy" several times, I gave up my protests. Jorge guided the chosen creature away, patting it on the rump with his machete as he walked beside it. I grabbed the other blade and went back to chopping wood, which allowed me to keep my back turned to the ordeal.

My eyes may have been averted, but nothing shielded me from the cries of the animal as it was slaughtered.

I froze, and over the shrieking and squeals—eerily humanlike—I heard some of the others in our group expressing their own disgust. Several of the boys began yelling at Jorge to finish the job, and I heard him yell, "I'm trying!"

Someone—I didn't see who—ran over and snatched the machete out of my hand and presumably used it to help out.

I cupped my hands over my ears and knelt in the moss wondering —and not for the first time—what was wrong with me. Why I felt like throwing up.

Tarsi came over and joined me; she wrapped an arm around my waist as we both knelt amid the scattered chips and splinters of wood. She held me until the sounds stopped, stroking my head and kissing my cheek.

Much of my initial shock came from pity for the poor animal—as frightening as the thing had seemed to me mere moments before. But it was my own shame at having such a strong reaction that left me suddenly feeling as if I weren't a part of the group.

Later, while the smell of the animal roasting over the fire drifted around our camp, I moved to a low spot in the tree's tunnel and ate raw bombfruit, feeling as sorry for myself as I did the dead vinnie.

"You sure you don't want some?" Kelvin asked when he came over to check on me.

"I'm positive," I said, thankful he was considerate enough to not come bearing a portion of the animal on a stick.

"You want to talk about it?"

I laughed at him and scooted over, leaving room in the tunnel for him to sit and swing his legs. "That's *my* line," I said.

Kelvin grunted. "Maybe *we're* the ones who're messed up." He nodded back toward the campfire.

I didn't accept his diagnosis, but it did make me feel better. I had a sudden impulse to rest my head on his shoulder, to let his strength prop me up similar to the way Tarsi often sank into mine. But I restrained myself.

"You and Tarsi have fun while we were gone?" he asked.

I looked over at him and saw his jaw muscles flexing as he clenched and unclenched it over and over. "Look, Kelvin—"

He reached his arm around me and squeezed my shoulder. "Hey, it's no big deal. It should be her choice, right?"

"No, listen to me—"

"I'm serious, Porter, it's fine. I'd rather her choose you than half these other guys."

"Only half?" I asked, smirking at him.

"Well, Karl is quite a bit better-looking than you—"

I punched his knee. "Seriously, though, I need to tell you something. I'm— It's stuff I'm just sorting out on my own. I don't even know how to say it without freaking you out—"

"Hey," he said, standing up and backing away, his hands held high. "I'm cool with you guys being together, but I don't wanna hear specifics, okay? And I don't know enough to give you advice, anyway."

"No, listen—"

But it was too late. Not just because Kelvin had backed toward the campfire, but because the impulse to spill my guts had passed.

Besides, there'd been quite enough of gut-spilling for one day.

Even as I abstained from the meat, I had to admit the smell was oddly intoxicating. My mouth watered at the odor of the roasting flesh, even as my brain rejected the idea of eating something dead. It was as if I'd skipped another training program. All I'd been prepared to eat was cultivated crops and protein mixes, but the other boys seemed to know without learning it that moving things were to be chopped up and cooked. And they also seemed to understand the best methods for doing both.

I finally rejoined the group as they finished eating, wary of ostracizing myself any further. Jorge made one probing jab at my manhood, but a look from Kelvin put a quick end to that. The other boys burped contentedly while the vinnies marched in a circle and my stomach continued to growl.

Eventually, we began considering our options aloud.

"Well, we certainly won't starve to death," Karl pointed out. "As long as the rains are steady, we'll be better off than those inside."

"The goal has to be more than that," I pointed out. When everyone turned to me, I clarified: "Beyond just 'not starving.'"

"You mean long term," Britny said. "Like I was saying the other day."

"Exactly. I mean building things. And finding a regular source of water, something to irrigate with."

"We discussed that on the way down," Kelvin said. "Vincent was thinking we could hack away some of the canopy up top and rig up tarps to the tunnel. Most of the rain doesn't even make it to the bottom. It's all puddled up there on top. We could create a massive flow of it down here, like a river spiraling down."

"That still relies on the rains," I said. "We've been awake for most of a month, and Colony's told us very little about the planet—"

"Are you thinking of the snow on the mountains?" Tarsi asked.

I nodded. "There must be streams from the runoff. Maybe we should think about—"

"Who made *you* the boss?" Jorge asked, leveling his machete at me from the other side of the fire.

"Nobody," I said. "I'm just asking questions—"

"Sounds like you're making plans," he said, then made a show of tearing off a bite from a cold piece of meat.

"Jorge, give it a rest," Tarsi said.

"Porter's right," Kelvin said. "Peter was trained as a farmer, like me. He may have been thinking the same thing."

"I don't want to go chasing after Peter and Mica on a hunch," Jorge said. "Besides, who needs farming when we can corral a bunch of vinnies? Right, Vinnie?"

"We can't keep calling them that if we're gonna keep eating them," Vincent said, frowning.

"Agreed," Britny said, putting her arm around Vincent. Several of us nodded as well.

"Making any decision is gonna to be impossible like this," Samson said. "Who here is ranked the highest?"

"I don't wanna get that kind of hierarchy going out here," I told the group.

Karl pointed at me. "Guess we know who's ranked the *lowest*," he said.

Everyone laughed, and I had to join in. He smiled to let me know no harm was meant.

"I'm actually the lowest," Samson admitted. Several of us already knew that, as he was open with the fact that he'd been in the vat right next to the exit on our birthday, and consequently the first one out. "And I don't think she's gonna say anything, but Mindy is probably the highest. Her vat was by Myra's."

We all turned to her, and I saw her face grow redder than any of the sunburned boys.

"I refuse to lead this rabble," she said, smiling. "I'm just happy enough not to be mixing propellant for that rocket."

"Speaking of which," Tarsi said, "does anybody have a clue about why we were building that thing?"

Nobody answered.

"Should we care?" Britny asked.

"I think we should care about why this planet was deemed non-viable," Tarsi said.

"Lack of metal," Leila said. "Besides gold," she added.

"That's the rumor," said Kelvin, "but you sound like you know something."

"I know who started the rumor," Leila said. "Mica told me about it. She's a geologist, so it could be her bias, but I think she knew what she was talking about. Anyway, everything else about this place is perfect for life—just not good for building more colony ships and sending them off to other planets."

"That can't be it," Karl said. "They wouldn't abort us just because it's nice here but not profitable."

"You sure about that?" Leila asked.

Jorge sneered at me. "What do you think, Porter?"

I felt my body flush with heat as a wave of faces turned my way. I took a deep breath and peered into the fire.

"I think the lack of metals makes this a pretty poor planet for colonization. I tend to agree with Leila and Mica on this. But I also think we need to keep our minds open to something else. There could be seasonal weather we don't know about, or larger predators. And even though none of us signed anything, our births within the colony make us implicitly a part of a legal structure we've now turned our backs on. If the colony does do well, we're always gonna be outlaws. Besides—and I don't mean to be crass—if we don't have three kids per couple, none of this really means anything beyond our temporary happiness, right?"

"I call Britny," Jorge said.

Several of the boys laughed, but not Vincent.

"Fuck you, Jorge," Britny spat.

"You heard that, right?" he said. "That's a verbal agreement."

Everyone laughed even harder, except for Britny and me. Vincent glowered at Jorge, and Tarsi reached her hand through my arms and intertwined her fingers with mine. I looked over and saw she wasn't laughing either.

"So, have we all agreed to pair off and go roll around in the moss tonight?" Samson asked.

Mindy was closest to him, so it was left to her to slap his arm.

"I say we forget about the colony by putting some distance between it and us," Tarsi offered. "Let's pretend the day we squeezed through the perimeter fence was our real day of birth and the horrors beforehand were some final training we shared together."

The joking fell silent as we mulled that over. I really loved the beauty of the analogy, the ability to pretend the worst of my life had been as unreal as all before it. It reminded me of Myra's method of coping with the loss of Stevens.

"I also think we should try and find Mica and Peter," she said. "If they went toward the mountains, that also works for finding fresh water and getting away from the colony. It's the best of everything."

"I second that," Britny said.

A chorus of agreement followed. I squeezed Tarsi to let her know how much I supported the plan, and also how much I appreciated her deflecting the burden of leadership away from me.

"Well, then," Vincent said, "I have an idea on how we should get there."

"Besides walking?" Mindy asked.

"Now that you mention it . . . yeah, maybe. I was thinking we should hike back up to the canopy and walk across in a straight shot. It'll take forever to work our way around the trees."

"No way," Leila said. "And risk falling to our death?"

"It's not like that," Samson said. "The leaves are so packed and stiff, it's like walking on solid ground."

"Except it's two thousand feet *above* solid ground," one of the girls complained. "And it's a long way up to hike."

"Once the rest of you see the sky up there, you'll understand."

"Yeah," Jorge said. "Besides, I think Mindy had a good idea."

"I did?"

"Yeah. About not walking. Maybe we can ride the vinnies up!"

We all turned to look at the large creatures, who continued to worm their way around the small circle — an unending column of dark, shivering fur.

"We really gotta call them something different," Vincent said. "It's creeping me out."

20

UP

"EXCRUCIATING" DIDN'T QUITE COVER IT. THE HIKE up the gradual incline felt more like a stroll along death's edge. It only took half an hour for my legs to become sore, then my lungs started burning, and every step required concentration and brought pain. Even if I hadn't been overworked and half-starved from the previous weeks, the unending upward stroll would've severely taxed me. I like to think it would've taxed anyone.

Several others offered to walk while I rode a vinnie, but I felt as right about that as I did about eating them. The other colonists rode their backs, some of them in pairs. The girls squealed at first as the follicles of hair squirmed against them, but they eventually settled down. I chose to hike at the back of the column, pausing now and then to appreciate the views while gasping for breath. The saving grace with the vinnies was their plodding pace. I could walk and catch up, stop to suck down precious oxygen, then repeat. I tried conserving my water, but we looked to be a mere quarter of the way up by the time I'd drunk half my supply, which forced me to ration it even more judiciously.

Lunch had to be eaten on the move, as even without the chip dangling in front of the lead vinnie, they didn't seem to know how to stop. Tarsi dropped off the back of her vinnie and joined me. There was plenty of cooked meat left over; I knew she would prefer to have some of it, but she shared my bombfruit instead. We walked and ate in silence, my lungs hardly up for the hike, much less a conversation while I staggered along.

A few hours after lunch, my legs and lungs were too shot for me to maintain my ethical stance. There was no way I was going to be able to stay with the group unless I took a ride and rested myself. After I admitted my defeat, Britny moved off the rear vinnie and joined one farther up, leaving me room to join Tarsi. She dropped off and walked beside me, coaxing me along as I huffed and puffed and tried to mount the animal.

"You have to grab the fur," she told me.

I wanted to tell her I was trying but got out nothing more than a wheeze. The way the fur waved, it seemed like its skin was in motion, as if the beast were a living conveyor belt. I tried to keep in mind that the fur along its back wasn't really being used for locomotion — that it was just the ends waving. I kicked myself for being a wimp and decided to just grab, pull, and apologize.

I lunged over the back of the vinnie, trying to give more than a halfhearted effort as I grabbed some of the moving bristles. The rest of the fur wiggled across my stomach, sending shivers up and down my spine. I had to hold on pretty tight, or the pushing movement of the hair would've sent me right off its ass and onto mine.

Tarsi pushed at my feet, urging me forward. I let go with one hand and reached up for another hold farther up. Pulling myself along, I felt the hair beneath me bend in the other direction and the wiggling begin to *assist* me as I moved up the beast's back. When I reached the rope circled around its featureless neck, I took hold of it and wiggled side to side the way Tarsi had said to, dispersing the hair in either direction.

With my belly right on the vinnie's back, it didn't feel quite as creepy as I thought it would. And not once did the creature seem to notice my weight, neither swaying nor slowing. Tarsi grabbed my calf, then thigh, then pulled herself up until her chest rested on my back, her breath playing across my neck.

"Is that so bad?" she asked.

It wasn't, and I tried to catch my breath to admit it.

Tarsi left her hands on my shoulders. I felt her head turn sideways and rest on the top of my spine. I shifted my head in the other direction to look away from the center of the tree and out at the world moving by. Every few feet, we crept behind one of the jutting outcroppings of bark and our world descended into darkness. Then we would pop out into daylight as the cylindrical tunnel broke through the exterior of the tree at the bases of the cog-like indentations. It was like passing row upon row of open windows, each one providing a beautiful glimpse of the clearing below. In the distance, I could see more trees across a clearing smaller than the one our base occupied. In half a day, we had gone around the perimeter of the tree three times—if I had counted the passing of our wide clearing correctly.

"How many times do you think we go around to get to the top?" I asked Tarsi.

"I asked Kelvin the same thing. They thought it was ten or twelve times."

I hugged the vinnie, as appreciative of its service as I could be. "This isn't too bad," I told Tarsi, who squeezed my shoulders in response.

Sometime later, I startled awake to find the tunnel shaded in dusk. I hadn't even meant to go to sleep. The rhythmic swaying of the vinnie beneath me must've knocked me out.

Letting go of the rope collar with one hand, I rubbed my eyes and looked out below, where large branches reached out of the trunk and up toward the canopy. My shifting seemed to wake Tarsi, who kissed me on the back of the neck and said she needed to stretch.

Her body slid off mine as if dragged backwards. I lifted my chest and allowed the hairs of the creature to stir beneath me. As soon as I pushed back slightly, the vinnie did the rest, its fur carrying me down its back and right off its rump.

I landed roughly on my hands and knees and tried to stand, my legs still half-asleep.

"How long were we out?" Tarsi asked.

"You're asking *me?*" I stretched my back before setting off after the lumbering vinnies. "I'm pretty sure I fell asleep before you did."

Tarsi grabbed my hand and pulled me toward the edge of one of the outcroppings. We gazed out at the land below, my sense of direction destroyed by the nap and the looming darkness.

"Looks like more of those big pits in the ground out there," Tarsi said, pointing to perfectly circular dots scattered across the verdant green.

"That limb is massive," I said, pointing out and to the side.

"I hope that means we're close."

I joined her in looking up, but it was hard to judge how far away the canopy was. "Let's keep up with the others," I said, losing sight of the back of the train in the dim light.

We walked at the rear for almost half an hour, and my lungs and legs started to burn again. Somehow, though, the pain and tiredness weren't as scary as before, having survived it once. Plus, the psychological boost of knowing I could get on the vinnie at any time prevented any panic from setting in. It was the panic that made the tiredness transform into exhaustion.

As it grew even darker outside, I took to dragging one hand against the inner wall as I held Tarsi's tightly with the other. Then, without warning, exhaustion seemed to overtake me, and my legs began shaking uncontrollably.

"I think I need to go lie dow—"

Before I could finish the thought, the tree began to move beneath my feet, nearly throwing me to the ground. Beside me, Tarsi's arms swung wildly, and her hand slipped out of my own. I heard her scream, her voice moving away from me and toward the open air of one of the gaps in the bark and the great plummet beyond. Reaching out, groping for her in the darkness, I felt our hands touch several times — the moment of panic stretching out into an eternity of dread. I touched her sleeve, grabbed it, and yanked her close, both of us falling to the floor of the tunnel.

"What's going on?" she yelled.

A symphony of whistles grew outside, the sound of hundreds of bombfruit streaking through the air. I almost got out of my mouth that it was another earthquake when our vinnie crashed into us, his thistles moving in reverse, powering him down the tree.

Tarsi and I kept hold of each other as the large creature squeezed between us. We clutched with both hands and formed a human bridge over his back as the movement of the hair beneath us tried to propel us up the tree and toward the vinnie's head.

Higher up the spiral, someone started yelling, telling us to stop the vinnies. In the dim light filtering through the open side of the tunnel, I could see the next vinnie close on the heels of the other, the entire train moving in reverse. When the break in the chain reached us, I pulled Tarsi to my side, getting her away from the open air. The second animal passed, someone on its back yelling at it and then at us. Behind me, I could feel the tree shivering, the coarse wood vibrating against my spine.

"We have to wait it out," I told Tarsi, yelling over all the other people's shouts.

Another vinnie passed with someone hurrying along beside it, hugging the inner wall. The form bumped into me before I could move out of the way or warn them.

"Porter?" A face leaned in close to mine.

"Karl? What the hell, man? How do we stop them?"

"Screw it," he said. He grabbed my arm as the tree continued to vibrate. "We're almost there. Plenty more where those—"

A rumble cut him off, a sound like grinding, splintering wood. It wasn't the noise of the tremors, and it completely drowned out the whistling of the bombfruit. We all froze, except for the vinnies, which seemed to double their speed. They brushed past us, carrying a rider or two along with them as the noise grew louder, drawing near.

21

FALLING STAR

THE LAST VINNIE SQUEEZED PAST MY SHINS, AND A cluster of my friends followed, pushing, shoving, and falling down in the process. A few tried crawling over the back of the last vinnie, which was moving in reverse and at a brisk pace. I heard one of the guys yelling for us to run, but there was nowhere we *could* run, and no visible sign of danger. I peered up where the dark gray of dusk faded to black in the tunnel's depths. The curvature of the massive tree was so slight, we normally could see a good distance ahead. Now we just saw a hollow void made indiscernible and frightening by the shaking of the tree and the roar of something destructive.

Beside me, Karl cursed and grabbed my arm. That's when I saw it as well: a wall of blackness drawing near — something coming for us, its bulk filling the entire width of the tunnel.

The three of us ran after the others, tripping over people as we went. I tried to keep in touch with Tarsi, but I had no idea whom I was holding. As the tree moved beneath our feet, we took turns falling, helping each other up, and fighting the urge to look over our shoulders.

I didn't need to. I could hear it drawing near, the sound of splitting wood accompanying its approach.

"Over the side!" one of the girls shrieked, and at first I thought she meant someone had fallen or had been shoved out through one of the openings in the tunnel. Then I felt the person next to me stop scrambling and move up the outer curve and out into the night air. There were fewer of us running and crawling, and the thing kept getting closer, the splintering noise so loud I could barely hear everyone else yelling and screaming.

I groped for Tarsi and felt someone move out through the next opening. As soon as I realized what they were doing, I knew it was our only choice.

"Hold the edge!" I yelled to the person beside me. We stumbled past the next cog together, moving from pitch-blackness to the thick gray of one of the openings. We both crawled over the edge. My feet scratched at the rough bark as I lowered myself, allowing my armpits to catch on the sharp lip of the tunnel where its curve rose up and met the air. With my head still in the cylinder, I looked over and saw the loud darkness upon us — a wall of moving black and shivering power. I popped my elbows free of the edge and fell a foot before the tunnel's sharp lip bit into my fingers. I dangled there, my legs kicking above a thousand feet, maybe two, of nothingness.

Something rough brushed across my knuckles, nearly knocking my hands loose. Then the body went past, the large bristles poking out of the tunnel as a vinnie the size of the hole — or bigger, judging by the sound of crushed wood — tore past. Up and down my chest, I could feel the tree quaking. With the vibrations and the pressure on my fingers, maintaining my grip felt impossible. It was too much to ask of my body.

Still, I managed to yell encouragement to my neighbor. "Hold on!" I told them, hoping my urgency would provide strength, even if my words held no advice beyond the obvious.

A deep voice shouted something back, the voice of a male.

My heart sank and my stomach lurched, the two organs colliding within me as my guts reacted to the confusion in my head. I wanted Tarsi to be out there with me—was glad she wasn't—but wondered if she was someplace worse. I ground my teeth together and rested my head against the rough bark, feeling it scratch my forehead as it continued to shake.

After what seemed to be a full mile of quivering beast passed by, I flexed my arms to scramble up, then heard another coming. I relaxed, allowing my weight to dangle from my joints rather than my muscles, and thought about what the fall would be like. I pictured the tumbling descent, my body bouncing between the walls of the juts and hitting the moss far below. I thought about my existence winking out and being no more, ever again.

Bristles pushed against my hand, and a bombfruit whistled nearby. The guy beside me kept cursing loudly, but I had no encouragement within me to loan him. Then, the shaking of the tree stopped, leaving just the rumble of the enormous vinnie. I felt the numbness in my joints go away and realized much of it had been from the vibrations. If that was the last of the beasts, I could make it.

And if I could, maybe we all could.

As the final bristles passed, I tried pulling myself up, preferring that I be swallowed or crushed by the next vinnie rather than fall to my death. Pressing my feet against the bark—one foot on the outcropping to my side—I made it up to my armpits, then took a break, my hands clasped together and my elbows spread wide. The guy beside me did the same, our legs brushing together as we both fought for purchase.

In the downward distance, the rumbles from the jumbo vinnies receded, and no new ones took their place. I felt a nervous laughter creep up inside, the exhaustion and mania of near-death popping in my brain like tiny bubbles. The person beside me started before I could, wheezing and laughing—

Then someone screamed.

A high voice. A girl's voice. It pierced the growing quiet like a sharp dagger through a healing wound. It was a shriek as loud as any I'd ever heard, but then it sickeningly—horribly—began receding into the distance.

Growing silent.

Falling away.

22

THE DARKNESS

I KICKED AT THE SURFACE OF THE TREE AND PUSHED myself up to my waist. I leaned over, half my body through the hole. With another shove, I rolled myself all the way in. The guy beside me came hurrying after. I moved quickly down the tunnel, groping at the next opening, and felt someone move inside the tunnel and help their neighbor up.

"Tarsi!" I yelled. I patted my way down the line, wondering if the sound had come from the other direction, when I bumped into more bodies. I felt lost, alone, confused.

"Who *was* that?" someone yelled.

"What the *fuck?*" screamed another. I tripped over someone lying across the tunnel, patted them, then screamed Tarsi's name again, selfishly unconcerned about everyone else.

Others did likewise, yelling out individual names as they tried to make contact with each other in the darkness.

"Porter!" someone shouted nearby—a gruff shout. I felt strong hands clasp my arm, pulling my face close enough to see.

Kelvin.

"Where's Tarsi?" I asked.

He shook his head, and I read it to mean that she didn't make it, not that he didn't know. Someone screamed for help farther down the tunnel. I pushed away from Kelvin and moved to the next opening; I dropped to my knees and patted along the lip with my hands.

I felt knuckles and reached down for the wrists, my fear of losing another person rising up like a film of metal in my throat. Kelvin landed beside me and fumbled for the other arm. Together, we pulled. I willed my tired and numb fingers to close like a vise, fully prepared to never use them again if it meant dragging that person to safety.

Whoever it was kicked with their feet to help. The fearful energy of all three of us propelled the person over the lip and inside, sending us all flying back toward the core of the tree. We crashed in a heap of quivering, tearful humanity.

Hands groped, discerning identity. A palm on my cheek, a face brought near.

Tarsi.

I closed my eyes and wept, sobbing like a terrified child. Her lips fell to my cheek and stayed there, quivering against me, panting and gasping. Both of our bodies shook with grief, with exhaustion, and with guilt-ridden relief.

23

A LONELY PATCH OF SKY

OUR GROUP COALESCED IN THE DARKNESS LIKE beads of water. We bumped, hugged, wept, and merged together. We called out our own names and those of our neighbors, working through the list in our heads. Now and then, a name was spoken and someone else cried out, crawling over the rest of us to be reunited.

It seemed we heard each name twice before someone realized who was missing.

"Britny," someone whispered, her name said in a manner unlike the rest. It was an answer, rather than a question.

Several girls wailed. I heard Vincent shouting obscenities beside me and reached out for him in sympathy.

Our entire group formed into a ball of consoling hands, patting and squeezing. The scene was so eerily like our birthday, but the fear and grief were so much stronger now, having spent so many waking hours together.

"We need to get out of here," one of the guys said.

"We just lost someone!" one of the girls shrieked.

"He's right," a soft voice said, as sobs turned into sniffles. "It isn't safe in here. If another one comes, I can't do it again."

"Up or down?" someone asked.

Beside me, Vincent roared. I heard flesh slapping against flesh, and I moved to break it up—I felt him striking his own face.

"Stop it!" I told him, wrapping my arms around his shoulders. "We survive to mourn her properly."

His hands went to the back of my head, pulling our cheeks together. I felt his chest moving in and out with quiet sobs and felt someone else's hands reach around us both.

"Up," someone said. "It's closer, and it's away from the ones that just passed."

"Maybe they reverse direction when the tremors stop."

"The tremors stopped a while ago."

In the silence that followed, we gathered our courage and our wills and trudged upward.

We staggered forward as a tight group, hands against the inner wall and on each other. I made Tarsi walk inside of me, not able to stand the thought of her anywhere near the edge.

Kelvin walked ahead of us. I rested a hand on his shoulder, needing to maintain contact for more than just finding my way. We moved in complete silence, save for the occasional whistle of a bombfruit outside and the unexplained, unprompted curse from various members of the group.

I tried not to shuffle my feet, lest I pick up splinters from the newly exposed wood. I felt exhausted and depressed, a sensation that seemed to come after working so hard to stay alive. It was as if my body had exhausted all its energy—its desire to preserve itself. Now that it had succeeded in doing so, extending my life for however much longer, there was no more of that juice within me to maintain my will to live.

Consciously, I was happy to be breathing and for my two dearest friends to be alive. But physically, I felt hollow. If another danger posed itself, I would lack the energy to respond. I was walking—but until that mysterious animus of self-preservation renewed itself, I was a staggering husk, half-dead inside.

We moved like that for several hours, the silence stretching out so long it began to sustain itself, the quietude forming into something fragile and precious that none of us seemed willing or able to shatter. Even when the tunnel diverted, heading off at an angle that seemed so foreign after the miles of gradual curving, those of us who had not made the prior ascent went along without question, accepting whatever the world threw at us.

Scrambling up a steepening slope, we fell to our hands and knees as it became too precarious to stand. The tunnel had become solid; having walls on all sides was oddly comforting despite the darkness it created. We passed another odd twist and the way became even steeper, and then there was the sound of rustling up ahead. Something like waxy paper brushed across my face. A leaf? The cave of wood ended, as did the silence.

"Careful," one of the guys whispered.

Hands guided hands through the new tangle of limbs and dried leaves around us. Something about grasping the boughs with my palms and the upward climbing felt completely natural. Primal. I pushed Tarsi up behind Kelvin and followed so near to her that my hands clutched holds above her feet, my head brushing against the backs of her legs. We seemed to be climbing up a hole in the tight weave of limbs, a continuation of the cave that bore through the canopy. It almost went vertical, and I could feel people climbing up behind me, all of us spreading out and fighting to reach the end. We were powered along by some intense internal desire to be safe. To rest.

I felt as if we would soon break free, but the tunnel through the tangled wood began to level out. Then it descended slightly, and I felt a moment of panic, wondering if we still had a long way to go. The branches underfoot became damp as the ground dipped down, then gradually rose back up. There was more rustling ahead, and someone above us cried out. A thick flap of leaves was pushed aside, and a crisp light filtered down through the darkness. I immediately felt the energy around me—*within* me—grow. The sense of finality swelled, the end so tantalizingly near.

When Tarsi and I at last reached the lip of the opening, Kelvin pulled us out. The three of us collapsed with the others on top of a flat spread of foliage, where we lay on our backs in a new silence of hushed awe. Above us hung a sight we were vaguely familiar with from years of dreaming but had never before seen with our own eyes: a wide tapestry of blackness speckled with pinpricks of brilliant light.

Stars. Countless stars. Bright and shimmering. Chaotic yet somehow ordered. Different, yet the same. Some seemed so much closer than others, and some were clumped together in tight packets of camaraderie. One third of the sky was especially dense, a wide band of white dots so intermingled, they seemed fuzzy as they stretched from horizon to horizon.

"Holy shit," one of the guys whispered, a reminder to the girls and me that they hadn't seen this either.

I tore my eyes away from the view and surveyed our group, thankful for the collected illumination from all those distant suns. I wondered if we were lucky for so many of us to have survived, or *un*lucky to have been so close to the top before it all happened. One of the girls moved over and embraced Vincent, whispering her condolences. Tarsi squeezed my hand, and I reached for Kelvin with the other. My chest hurt with the thought of losing either of them.

In the distance, I saw shapes moving, a train of vinnies sliding across the pale green carpet of the canopy. Looking around, I noticed many more of them and saw the leaves rustling here and there as the large beasts burrowed down into the leaf-ground or reappeared from below. It was an alien landscape, I thought, even as I reminded myself that it was the only home I'd ever known. Nothing in the training modules had prepared us for this. And when I thought about the presence of so much air beneath me—separating us from the hard earth below—I felt faint. Like we were floating on a cloud and willing its firmness to hold.

Without a word—just a soft chorus of sobs—our little group tightened, our bodies pressing together like our first night outside the fence. Hands interlocked with other hands, no care for whom they belonged to.

They were all ours.

All squeezing.

All loving and all fearful.

I rested my head on someone's arm and gazed up at the stars, watching them twinkle through my tears, as mesmerized by the complete blackness between them as I was by their light. I soon found one patch that was startlingly devoid of anything, a lonely little patch, and I lost myself in it, drifting off to nothing.

24

THE BLUE

I SLEPT BETTER THAT NIGHT THAN I HAD REASON TO and woke to a sight far happier than any of us expected: open sky—the sun washing out the black and most of the stars. It replaced them with a dull gray that started on one horizon and faded to a bright blue on the other. Sunrise. I could feel myself reading something mystical into it, like an apologetic gesture from the heavens for having to take one of our number away. As that sensation stirred within me, I found myself thinking of Oliver. I began to understand him, if only a little —mainly his seemingly irrational grope for joy in times of hardship.

Our sleeping tangle had loosened overnight as some of us tossed and turned and tried to get comfortable. I brushed Tarsi's hair off her forehead and kissed her softly above the brow, so thankful nothing had happened to her. She stirred, her lips parting slightly, but didn't wake. I worked my arm free and pushed away from the group, the ache in my joints demanding movement; or perhaps it was something in my jittery thoughts that made me feel compelled to force myself into motion.

I was the only one up. Not even the vinnies stirred as they had the night before. Turning to look for them, I felt overwhelmed with the vast sameness stretching out before me, the undulating carpet of several varieties of overlapping green leaves. Some of them were larger than a man with his limbs spread wide; some were small as my hand, dark green, and just as thick. When I spun halfway around and saw the mountains behind me lit up by the rising sun, my breath caught in my throat.

I knew what mountains looked like, just as I knew of earthquakes and guns and kisses. But once more, reality shattered concept. Majestic, towering pyramids of earth rose up beyond the canopy, their tops slathered in snow and tinged pink by the morning sun. The peaks were arranged in countless layers, each fading through various hues of blue until the farthest receded into purple. They seemed to stretch off into a forever that made the green carpet in the opposite direction pale by comparison. They even dwarfed the majestic trees, which had already upset my innate sense of scale.

A cool breeze drifted across the treetops from the west, the air seemingly chilled by the mighty blocks of ice-topped granite. They could have been a thousand miles away or ten, my sense of distance was so completely obliterated. Between the last glimmer of morning stars above, and the size of the leaves beneath me, the mountains provided one last blow to my ego—my sense of belonging to this universe—and made all else seem insignificant by comparison.

"It's gorgeous," Tarsi whispered. Her arms encircled me from behind, and I rested my hands on top of hers, feeling a joy from our contact that somehow grounded me from the enormity of my surroundings.

"I can't believe she's gone," I said, thinking of Britny. I wanted to say *I wish she could have seen this,* but it felt too trite and sad to utter. Tarsi replied by squeezing me. I felt her chin find a sore muscle in my back, her head sagging and heavy against me.

"We were supposed to *conquer* this?" I heard her whisper with sadness.

The thought stirred something within me. Something angry. Then it floated off on the freshening breeze, lost among the gentle flapping of blanket-sized leaves.

* * *

It didn't take long for the growing light to wake the others. While everyone took in the amazing sights to all sides—the boys reveling in our delight as we saw it for the first time—a gradual giddiness seemed to conquer our loss. All except for Vincent, who remained silent and detached despite our efforts to include him.

Part of me felt guilty for taking excitement in anything, and we all seemed to pay homage to his greater sadness by tempering our enthusiasm. When one of us accidentally laughed or grew excited, a sheepish, apologetic look tended to follow.

We sorted through the gear that had survived the previous night's ordeal, several of us bemoaning the loss of a precious item: a thermos, a strip of canvas, even an entire pack. We inventoried what was left, none of us speaking a word on what Britny had been carrying even though I'm certain we were all silently, guiltily, tallying her things.

The girls broke out what remained of the cooked vinnie meat while Karl and Samson crawled back down into the tree to search for dangling bombfruit. We rationed our water carefully, the brilliant blue sky overhead a refreshing novelty and also a cloudless curse.

"We should have known that was a possibility," Kelvin said, plopping down beside me and shaking his head. "Why would the tunnel be that size unless they came that big?"

"Yeah." I nodded and picked splinters out of my calloused feet.

"You think those were the adults? Is that as big as they get?"

I shook my head. "I don't know. Or it's a male-female thing." I glanced up to see several others following our conversation in silence while they toyed with their food.

"How do we get down?" Mindy asked me. Once again, faces turned my way, even though I'd shown no particular aptitude nor willingness to lead. I dwelt on this tendency of the group to ask my opinion when what I should've been doing was thinking of an answer for Mindy. I wondered if it was nothing more than Stevens taking me aside that first day, or maybe the fact that only my flashlight had survived our es-

cape. I bit my lip and mulled whether it would be best to put an end
to whatever shred of authority I seemed to hold among the group, or if
my even hesitating threatened to fill them with despair.

"Where's the sign from Mica and Peter?" I asked Jorge, hoping to
deflect the burden to someone more eager to shoulder it.

"Below," Samson said, intercepting the question. "Right past that
dip in the brambles. It pointed that way." He gestured toward the nearest peaks.

"How long do you think we can last up here?" Leila asked.

"Without rain? Not long," Kelvin said. "I say we head toward the
mountains and scout below the canopy now and then. There have to
be rivers flowing down from that snow and from the rain."

"Yeah, but how do we find a way *down?*" Mindy asked. "How do we
get past those *things?*"

"We can mark the tunnels when they come out at night," Karl said.
"We'll gather some more up in a circle using the thick leaf chips they
like. Maybe we'll lead them ahead of us, just in case the canopy is thin
in places."

"But *then* what?" someone asked. "We head back down? Just take
our chances?"

"Maybe it was the tremors," I said. "It could've been a fluke."

"Don't call it a fluke," Vincent said, not looking up.

An uncomfortable silence ensued.

"I'm sorry," I told him.

He waved his hand. I wasn't sure how to interpret the gesture.

"We'll go down as before," Kelvin said, rescuing me. "We'll lead a
long train of vinnies down ahead of us. They seemed to know something was coming. The more of them we have, the more warning we'll
get."

"Good idea," Tarsi said.

"We could cut some long sticks from the brambles," Mindy said.
"We'll sharpen them in case we need to drive them back."

"Even if that doesn't work, if they were long enough to span the gaps in the tunnel, they'll make it easier to hang on if we have to go over the edges again."

"Especially if we rigged up bits of rope on them for our wrists."

Kelvin and I looked to one another as the group started spouting out suggestions. I raised my eyebrows, signaling my appreciation for his help as a growing sense of purpose took hold of our group. The urge to survive seemed to be returning, bringing with it the motivation to move forward.

Wherever that took us.

25

THE STORM

I TOOK THE LEAD AS WE SET OUT ACROSS THE CAN-
opy, my comparatively diminutive size making me the least likely boy
to go crashing through a soft spot or one of the dozens of vinnie passages down into the trees. Tarsi had tried to insist on walking along beside me, but neither I nor Kelvin would hear of it. The two of them
followed a dozen paces behind, trying to include me in their sporadic
conversations.

The tight weave of branches and thick layer of leaves made for a rel-
atively comfortable walk. When a stiff wind rolled through the trees,
the canopy beneath us seemed to sway ever so slightly. It filled my
stomach with a sickening sensation I might liken to being on a sailing
ship or bounding across a small moon. I'd never done either of those
things, of course, but both somehow seemed less alien to me than hiking across a treetop.

The terrain ahead was full of bumps and dips, including some very
long ridges that seemed to indicate major branches underneath. I stuck
to those, not just for the promise of stability but to stay out of the small
puddles of warm water that had collected in the valleys. A quick taste
led to even quicker spitting, though someone suggested it could be
boiled and made safe. The few vinnies we saw in the daylight seemed

to prefer these lower areas, especially any that dipped down far enough to provide shade.

When the ridges petered out and I had to cross over a lower spot, I did so carefully, testing my weight on one foot before shifting the other forward. After a few of these crossings without incident, I stopped being so conservative.

And that's when my leg crashed through the canopy.

It happened so fast, I never felt any sense of danger. There was a loud crack of snapping wood, and then I was on my butt, my entire leg hanging through a hole in the canopy. Kelvin slid forward on his belly and pulled me back. I was safe and it was all over before I even really knew it was happening. But it made us all more cognizant of the dangers we had to be aware of on this trek.

Exploring around the thin section, we discovered another of the large tunnels beneath. We made our way around it and up to another ridge before stopping for a ration of water and some bombfruit.

While everyone else ate, Kelvin gathered every scrap of rope we had and began splicing them together. I watched him with mild curiosity as he looped both ends of the line and tied a series of complex knots.

He came over as I took my two sips of water and showed me his creation.

"What's that?" I asked.

"Your new leash." He held the rope up and snapped it tight a few times to demonstrate the general idea. "We both get to wear one end."

"I'll be fine," I told him. "That was a fluke back there. Besides, that thing will just pull you down after me."

He looked me up and down, and then laughed. "I don't think so," he said.

"He'll wear it," Tarsi said, grabbing the water pouch from me and taking a sip.

"Fine," I said, knowing better than to argue with both of them. I lifted my arms and let Kelvin lower the loop down around my waist. He cinched it tight, somewhere between nervous-tight and paranoid-

tight, then played out the line and worked the other loop around himself.

"You're welcome," he said to me, glancing up after he checked his
knots.

"Thanks," I said, feeling ridiculous.

"All the same, try not to fall through any more holes that would
have you plummeting to your death."

We set off again after everyone refreshed themselves. As the hours
passed, the heat of the overhead sun bore down unlike anything we'd
ever experienced. I took my shirt off and draped it over my head,
having seen what exposure to those rays had done to the boys who
had spent just a few hours at the top, and most of that with cloudy
skies.

Around noon, the vinnies started making more frequent appear-
ances. They popped up from the foliage and gathered by the warm
puddles or chewed contentedly at the thicker chips of leaves. All the
vinnies we saw were of the smaller variety—none like the ones that
had stampeded us and caused Britny's death.

Also making an appearance after noon was a dark band of clouds—
great billowy gray things that smothered the distant peaks and rolled
across the surface of the range. Verbally, we decided the clouds were a
good sign. Karl had sampled a few of the shallow puddles and agreed
with me that they didn't taste right. However, despite the relief of fresh
water and the cooling cover the clouds promised, I felt terrified at the
sight of so much *stuff* coming right for us. Especially as bolts of light
began flashing through the dark mass. A storm was brewing that managed to out-grumble my stomach.

"We'll need to find shelter before that gets here," Tarsi called up to
me. I watched the vinnies scurry about with greater urgency and wondered if we shouldn't start looking right then.

We hurried along, the danger ahead and above taking my mind
off the one below. I stopped picking my way as closely and no longer

tested my footing in the depressions. After half an hour of forgetful and impatient marching, I fell through the canopy. Completely.

It happened without a sound, just the swish of a giant leaf as it flopped down into one of the vertical caves. By the time Tarsi shrieked out, I had already crashed to the bottom, eight or so feet below, the rope coming tight against my armpits just as my knees landed on a slope of brambles. It was over before I could even feel a sense of danger. If anything, I just felt embarrassed for getting careless. I picked myself up, feeling for bruises, as Kelvin and Tarsi appeared above.

"Are you okay?" Tarsi asked.

I looked up. "I'm fine. Just feeling stupid."

More heads appeared around the hole as the rest of the group caught up.

"Maybe we should explore this one," Mindy said.

I grabbed the ladder of brambles ahead of me and began crawling out.

"I say we go until it gets dark or rains."

"Maybe this was a sign, though."

"Now you sound like Oliver."

I felt like saying something in his defense, then froze at the sound of a distant and faint rumbling.

"Quiet up there," I hissed.

A few people kept whispering, arguing about what to do with the rain coming.

"Keep it down," I begged. I lowered myself a few feet and pressed my ear to the brambles.

Kelvin bent his waist over the edge. He grasped the limbs above me and lowered his head down near mine. "What is it?" he whispered.

I held up my hand. It wasn't thunder, so my first thought was the beginnings of another earthquake, but it sounded too high-pitched and consistent to be that. The group above began laughing at something—drowning out the sound—and by the time Kelvin shut them up, the noise was gone or too faint to hear. We waited a second to see if it would come back, but the roll of distant thunder had me wondering if it had ever been there at all.

"Did you hear any of that?" I asked Kelvin.

He nodded, then pulled his head out of the hole.

"What was it?" Tarsi asked.

"Probably his stomach," Kelvin said. He reached his hand down for me. "C'mon," he said, helping me up.

After another few hours of hiking, the edge of the canopy finally came into view. The sun had begun moving behind the darkening clouds, which rumbled louder and more frequently as they approached. Only the base of the nearest mountain remained visible between the canopy and the storm, which forced me to concentrate on a single, jagged pattern of rocks to aim for, lest we begin walking in circles.

"End of the road up there," I said, stopping to allow the others to catch up. I watched as Karl and Mindy began gathering some of the chips the vinnies preferred while several others noted the location of a hole or two.

"Are you sure that's the edge?" Jorge asked, squinting ahead.

"Yeah, I can see it," Tarsi said, pointing past me.

"Why are we stopping here, then?"

"Because I don't want to keep walking while it thins out," I said. "Besides, think of the size of the clearings between the trees. We might be past the trunk of this one already."

There were grunts of accord, then Leila voiced a fear I think many of us shared: "What if there isn't a way down this tree?" she asked.

"Then we build a shelter up here," Kelvin said. "There's plenty of building material. There's food—and water coming. We'll keep exploring until we find something."

"Speaking of shelter, I just felt a spot of rain."

As if to punctuate the sentence, a large drop smacked a nearby leaf with an audible crack.

"We need to set up the tarps," Tarsi said. "I'm dying of thirst."

The clouds swallowed the last of the sun, and a premature darkness fell across the landscape. Fumbling with Kelvin's knots, I managed to loosen the safety rope and dropped it around my feet. I untied my shirt from around my waist and shrugged it back on, the chill setting in quickly.

"Let's camp here for the night," Mindy suggested.

"Agreed," said Karl.

The rain pattered down around us, and I cursed our stupidity for waiting so late to get settled. The rush of reaching the edge had interfered with good sense. Around us, dozens of the smaller vinnies began scampering to and fro, our constant companions seeming to react to the moisture. Only, instead of looking for shelter, their number appeared to be swelling.

"Looks like we're not the only ones getting thirsty," Tarsi said.

Leila pulled her tarp out of her pack. "Let's set these up to collect some water."

"Are they coming out of any one hole more than any another?" I asked.

"Karl and I saw a whole train coming out of one back there," Mindy said, pointing in the direction we'd come from.

"What are you thinking?" Kelvin asked.

"Just trying to find something that separates them. I feel like we're sitting on top of a maze, and I don't want to just start at random."

"And I don't want to get trampled," Jorge said.

"I'll go explore it," said Samson. Vincent agreed, and the two of them set off, but not before dropping their scraps of canvas and water containers.

"I say we set up close to their tunnel," Tarsi said. "We can take shelter in it while the water puddles."

We thought that was the best plan and followed the two boys back toward the hole. Meanwhile, hundreds of vinnies could be seen writhing across the landscape all the way into the distance. Tarsi stood beside me, watching them. "Almost feels like a party up here," she said.

"Yeah," Kelvin said, handing us one side of a tarp. "I just hope the grown-ups aren't invited."

26

DOWN

YET ANOTHER SLEEPLESS NIGHT ENSUED AS THE rain thundered down on the leaves above us. Our entire group had retired into the large tunnel Karl and Mindy had found, but it was impossible to sleep with the sporadic vinnie traffic and the rough tangle of woven limbs beneath us.

Kelvin and Samson went up onto the canopy once to cut some leaves away and bring them down for bedding, but the waxy surface was too slick to sleep on, thanks to the slope. And just like the major tunnel we had come up, the only flat dip in the upper section was soggy with collected water.

I rarely used the flashlight in order to conserve our only battery, which meant a night of damp and uncomfortable darkness. Whenever a vinnie would creep up from below, one of us would shriek in terror, causing the rest of the group to shift out of the way as it pushed itself up to the canopy. Nobody wanted to be the lowest person, the one the vinnies reached first, which resulted in a tight clump up where the slope was steepest. We clung to the brambles and one another, shivering and miserable.

We waited all night for the precious sun to come up. Minutes ticked by like hours. We took turns asking our neighbors what time they thought it was, but the answers were nothing more than guesses. I could feel the group growing restless, the reaction to a passing vinnie turning into anger rather than annoyance. Several times, Jorge crawled up and lifted the flap of leaves above us, poking his head out to look for the sun. After the fourth or fifth time, someone told him to give it up, as each peek just brought down a small shower of cold rain.

"I don't think it's coming," he said. "I think it's morning already, but the clouds are so thick the sun can't get through."

Looking up, I could see the faintest of silhouettes around me.

There did seem to be light filtering in from somewhere.

"I can't stand this," someone said.

"We need to just take our chances and go down. I'd rather be walking or riding a vinnie than sitting here like this."

"Agreed. My ass is cramping."

We all laughed at that, and the shared levity seemed to wake us up and signal the start of a new day — or at least the continuation of a very long one. As a group, I think we were still wary of the tunnels. Maybe that's why we were huddled up near the miserable rain, and why we shrieked whenever one of the smaller, harmless vinnies passed.

"Screw it," I heard one of the girls say. "I'm gonna go check on the water in the tarps."

"And I'm gonna head down," Karl said from directly below me. "Might as well explore this tunnel some." He said it like a question, with some lilt of doubt at the end like he needed to buttress himself. We were all silent for a moment, waiting to see if he would really do it.

Kelvin reached over and patted my arm. "Let's go with him."

I nodded, even though it was too dark for Kelvin to see me. Maybe I was just steeling myself, or perhaps I felt too anxious to fake the decision verbally. We followed Karl down to the soaked dip below us, all three of us likely feigning a confidence we didn't truly feel. One of the vinnies made its way past us, keeping high up the curved wall of the tunnel to stay out of the water.

"Vinnie coming," Karl shouted back to the rest.

I fumbled in my pack for the flashlight, even as each minute seemed to bring a tad more filtered light down through the canopy above. I flicked it on, and its bright cone revealed a tunnel similar to the one we'd ascended two days ago. The steep slant worked its way down through a dip before rising back up and falling down again.

I cursed myself for not using the flashlight the previous night when others wanted to explore further. We wouldn't have gotten any sleep with the vinnies passing through, but it might've been more comfortable on flat ground. *If* we could've gotten over our fears of what had happened the last time.

"It's like a plumber's trap," Kelvin said. He splashed forward into the puddle of water at the bottom, the level coming up past his ankles.

"A what?"

"The curved pipe below a sink," he explained.

"Like I know what those are for." I splashed past him, twisting up my nose at the smell of rot and mildew. Karl had already picked his way up the rise to where the tunnel leveled out again.

"It's to keep the rain out of the tunnels in the tree," Kelvin explained. "Whatever drips down from above collects in this low spot and leaks through the tangled limbs. The vinnies must've evolved the habit of chewing their tunnels this way."

"Or they're just smarter than they look," I said. A short train of vinnies crested the rise by Karl. I moved to get out of their way, but they swung to the side, up the slope of the tube and away from the water.

"They don't like to get their feet wet," Karl pointed out.

Kelvin and I followed as he continued forward, and I kept his way lit from behind with the flashlight. Several dozen paces farther and the tunnel began a gradual descent. We stumbled down until we came to one of the familiar openings in the gear-like side of the tree's trunk.

"Hell yeah," Karl said. He smiled back at us, his teeth flashing in my cone of light.

"Good call on picking this tunnel," Kelvin said, slapping my back.

I could feel myself beaming, even as I again lamented the less miserable night we could've had in the lower portion of the tunnel if only I'd agreed to go look. Then I thought about something bad happening, something like Britny, and realized it would've been my choice that *made* it happen. I had a sudden desire to hand the flashlight to Kelvin and run back, up to the treetop. I wanted to leave my decision-making behind, along with my responsibility for all future ones.

Kelvin and Karl knelt by the hole and looked out, oblivious to my fears. I crowded in behind them, resting my hand lightly on their shoulders so they wouldn't turn and bump into me—or get startled and fall.

Above us, the heavy patter of rain could be heard against the leaves, the *thwap*s of each impact ringing out like pops on a tight drum. Below, we could see the ground with far better clarity than we could see each other, as if the light of the world were *rising* instead of falling.

"We must be facing the mountains," I said. "The canopy's not blocking out the light in that direction."

Kelvin and I craned our necks to see more of the landscape, but a large limb rising up from below cut most of it off. I trained my light up the limb and toward the canopy, the falling rain sparkling as it streaked past. We could see dozens of bombfruit hanging from above, and it dawned on me that the rain we had felt back at base was nothing more than the delayed drippings from the real storms as the canopy leaked its puddles through its tight brambles.

Karl left us and walked down to the next few openings to see around the limb. He didn't get twelve feet away before he shouted back to us: "Fucking shit, guys. You've gotta see this."

Kelvin and I hurried down to join him, the three of us crowding along the edge of the opening. Karl pointed below, out past the far edge of the canopy's overhang where the rain fell heavy and unobstructed. Through the gray veil it created, out where dawn's storm-strained light seemed to surf down the face of the nearest mountain, we could see manmade things.

Colony things.

Two tractors were parked by a module, which sat in a distant circle of mud.

"It's gotta be the mine," Leila said as soon as we reported our findings to the rest of the group. All nine of us huddled below the entrance to the large tunnel, eating bombfruit cut from the underhang and drinking fresh rainwater.

"I thought this planet had a major mineral and ore deficiency. Are you saying Colony lied to us?"

"No," Leila said, shaking her head. "It's probably abandoned. How do you think Colony figured out there weren't any metals to begin with?"

"From the original mine," I said.

"Bingo."

"I think Colony even mentioned a mine site that first night," Tarsi said, "but it said the thing was a few days' drive away."

"Maybe it is. If you have to go around the trees, that is."

Kelvin wiped his mouth with the back of his hand and spoke around some bombfruit: "You think that's what Mica and Peter were heading toward?" he asked me.

"Maybe."

"What do you mean?" Jorge asked.

"Mica was interested in the mine," Kelvin said. "She and Porter talked about minerals or something one day over lunch." He looked to Leila. "And didn't you say she was a geologist?"

"Do you think she escaped to find something?" Leila asked me.

I shrugged. "I don't know what to think. Maybe—" I turned to Kelvin and snapped my fingers. "That rumble we heard earlier, when I fell through the canopy. I know what that was now."

"An engine," Kelvin said, his eyes wide. "A mining tractor?"

"I think Colony knows where Mica and Peter were heading. If that tractor is on its way, we need to get down there."

"Slow down," Jorge said. "If Colony's heading that direction, we need to stay up here, where we're safe. Besides, we still haven't talked about how we're gonna get down safely. We can't spend another day walking through these tunnels hoping another earthquake doesn't occur."

"I'm going down," I said to Tarsi and Kelvin, ignoring Jorge.

"Same here," Kelvin said. "I don't feel much safer up here. I need dirt under my feet."

Most of the rest of the group agreed, which left the question of how we would mitigate the dangers of the descent.

"I liked the idea of forming a long train of vinnies," Tarsi said. "That way we have a lot of warning. Besides, with the rainfall there's hundreds of them up here we could gather."

A drop of water smacked me on the top of my head; I could feel it worming through my hair and across my scalp. I looked up at the source of the drip, the dim light of the stormy morning finally filtering through the massive leaves. The drips had been tormenting me all night, filling my head with schemes, ways of keeping the moisture out completely. I couldn't blame the vinnies for crawling up the sides of the tunnel, trying to stay out of the wetness—

"I've got an idea," I said.

I scanned the group around me, their faces barely discernible and tinged with green. "Probably a stupid idea," I admitted.

Jorge snorted, obviously expecting no less.

"Let's hear it," said Kelvin.

The plan grew and altered as I spoke it. It began as a way to keep the vinnies out of the tunnel, but then it transformed into something crazy: a plan I began to doubt even as it formed. Everyone else just got excited and egged me on, which I suppose is how bad things tend to happen.

The allure of the idea was that we would be in the tunnel for as little time as possible, minimizing the chances of encountering another stampede-causing earthquake. A handful of us volunteered for the wet work, crawling out into the cold and working in the rain as it soaked us to the bone. Karl used one of the machetes to hack through the thick stems of the largest variety of leaves. The rest of us gathered them and passed them down into the tunnel. There, Kelvin and Leila carpeted the brambles with them, overlapping each leaf with the next as they created a nearly watertight flooring.

Meanwhile, using the other machete, Samson worked on the rise of the plumber's trap, cutting it out so the water could pass into the tunnel. As he chopped up the brambles, other workers passed the removed pieces along and tossed them through the gear holes farther down. Not only did this help remove the hump in the tunnel, the tossed limbs and hacked brambles would make for easy firewood if we could circle around the base of the tree and find them on the ground.

It took almost an hour to complete the work; by then, the rest of the group had rainwater funneling toward the large hole from the depression up top. The low valleys we had avoided while walking came into great use, collecting the rain and forcing it toward our tunnel. Using bits of sticks, we propped up the edges of some leaves to guide even more rain into the tunnel.

Once we were done, we gathered up the large leaves we had set aside and joined the others down past the flattened plumber's trap. The girls had already carpeted the area Karl had cut out, and a steady stream of water flowed through.

Those of us who had worked up top wrung out our clothes while the rest worked to secure our supplies. We distributed one big leaf per couple, with Kelvin agreeing to ride alone with a large tarp full of the majority of our gear.

As we worked, a train of vinnies marched past, all of them as high up the tunnel wall as their bristles could carry them. They were avoiding the rushing stream, just as I'd hoped.

Tarsi and I plopped down on the first leaf, the honor (and risk) of going first given to the person with the dumb idea. Below us, the floor of the tunnel gurgled with flowing water. I sat in front, straddling the stem of the leaf, both my hands on its forward edge and curling it back. Tarsi sat behind me, and we scooted forward, lurching the leaf inch by inch, while Kelvin and Samson shoved from behind.

At first, it felt like the entire endeavor would be a bust. I feared all of us had soaked ourselves to the core and worn ourselves out for nothing. Behind us, someone groaned as we struggled to get the contraption moving, but despite the waxiness of the leaf and the well-worn wood below, there seemed to be too much friction to get going.

Then—imperceptibly at first but growing—our scooting picked up speed. I could almost feel the bond between the leaf and wood slipping as the water eased us along. Behind me, Tarsi quit pushing and wrapped her arms around my waist. I leaned back and yelled for Kelvin and Samson to stop.

We were off. Moving at a walking pace for a few moments, and then faster. And faster.

"Whoa," Tarsi said, her grip around my chest making it difficult to breathe. I leaned back against her and concentrated on keeping the forward edge of the leaf up. Beside us, the openings in the tunnel flicked past. The rising curve of the round tube kept me from worrying about sliding out, and the tree was so large in diameter, it felt like we were going down a nearly straight chute rather than a tight spiral. The speed, however, quickly became a real concern. Within moments we were moving along faster than a tractor could go. I tried to keep my bearings with quick glances out the holes, but they flickered past so quickly, it was like seeing the world through rapid blinks.

"How're we gonna *stop?*" Tarsi yelled in my ear.

There were, admittedly, a few steps in my plan I hadn't fully mapped out.

I considered sticking my foot out against the core side of the tree, then thought about picking splinters out of my sole for the next week. Lowering the front edge of the leaf, I experimented instead with adjusting the shape of the curve, but couldn't tell that it had any effect. Continuing to unfurl it, I let part of the edge collapse completely, digging into the thin film of water. My reward was a furious spray of rainwater spitting right up in my face. Tarsi ducked behind me for cover, squealing, but our leaf definitely slowed. I played with it some more, then felt something bump into us from behind, nearly causing me to drop the edge of the leaf.

Tarsi squealed, and I heard someone grunt and cuss behind us: "Watch out!"

I turned around and saw Karl and Mindy right on our tail. Both had expressions of half-fear, half-exhilaration on their faces. Tarsi and Leila shouted back and forth, teasing one another.

"Stop fucking around and tell Karl to lower the front into the water," I hollered back to Tarsi. "Have him slow down and tell the next person."

She adjusted her grip on my waist and turned to explain it to the others. I kept the edge high and let go of the leaf with one hand to wipe the spray off my face and out of my eyes. We quickly picked up speed again, and I could hear Mindy's yelps of delight recede as Karl slowed his leaf down.

"This is fun!" Tarsi screamed, hugging my chest.

I laughed and tried to gauge our height off the ground to determine what our rate of descent was. Already, in my brief glimpses through the side of the tunnel, I could tell the canopy was receding overhead. I tried to get a read on the distance to the bottom. The best I could tell, we were already a good ways down. Maybe a tenth or so. A train of vinnies whizzed past on the core-ward side of the tree, and Tarsi and I leaned away as their bristles brushed against us.

"I wanna do this again!" she screamed in my ear.

I thought about the grueling climb up and shook my head. Then I recalled how nice the ride had been on the vinnie once I got over my objections and fears. I started to think that we could get up and down from the canopy without much difficulty—then I remembered the earthquake and the stampede. That returned me to my original doubts, and I promised myself I would never leave the ground again if I could just get back there safely.

What took almost a full day going up ended up taking less than two hours on the leaf. I watched the ground outside draw closer and lowered the forward edge, kicking up more spray and slowing us down. Tarsi groaned in my ear with disappointment.

Just before the end of the chute, we reached the edge of a large pool of water where the diverted rain had built up in the tunnel's dead end.

We jumped off our leaf and leapt out of the nearest hole, splashing down on the soaked moss. Karl and Mindy slid to a stop right as we got out of the way, laughing and wiping the spray off their faces. We helped them over the lip and stepped out into the dimly lit clearing. Two more riders arrived going much too fast; they slammed into the pool of water and sent spray out several gaps in the bark. Samson and Leila fell out the bottom of the tunnel, over a lip of cascading water, gasping for air and giggling uncontrollably.

Moving out into the rain, I opened the flap on my little canvas sack and peeked inside to make sure its contents had remained dry. Tarsi wrung water out of the bottom of her shirt, her hair plastered across her forehead.

I looked off in the direction of the mountains, but I couldn't see the mine from the lower elevation. What I *could* see was that we were in for a miserable camp . . . or a grueling, wet hike.

"What're we gonna do now?" I asked Tarsi.

She shrugged, then looked back toward the tree. "What's taking the others so long?" she asked.

27

TOGETHER

"SHOULD WE BUILD A SHELTER?" KARL TOOK A LEAF from Leila, who went back to the tunnel to fish out another. "Or should we try and get a fire going?"

"At least we're good on water," Mindy said, indicating the waterfalls spilling out of the last few gaps in the bark. The moss all around the base of the tree had turned into a small pond as it gathered the over-flow of water.

"Uh, about the water," Samson said. "I wouldn't drink it."

"Why not?" Leila asked, laying another leaf on the pile.

"It's, uh, not clean," he said quietly.

"What did you do?" Tarsi asked.

"I think I peed my pants a little . . ."

"You what?"

"When we passed that first vinnie," he mumbled, trying to defend himself. "Anyway, it wasn't much."

"That's so gross."

"I'm sorry."

"I was sitting right *behind* you," Leila complained.

"I said I was sorry."

Tarsi and I bent down to work with the leaves as we laughed at the exchange.

"Good thing we filled our water up top," she said to me. We each grabbed the sides of a leaf and tried to shape it into an upside-down "V," giving us a dry spot to stash our things. Unfortunately, the edges of the leaf were too flimsy and wet to stay put.

"I've got an idea," Tarsi said, running over and grabbing Karl's machete. She came back and sawed through the thick stem that ran the length of the leaf, breaking it but leaving the waxy surface intact. She bent the leaf right at the cut, sticking the end of the stem into the moss on one side and burying the tip of the leaf on the other. The stiffness of the stem kept both sides up, forming a tent of sorts, almost big enough for someone to ball themselves up under.

"Not bad," I told her, admiring the simplicity of it.

"It's better than not bad," she said, her hands on her hips, rain dripping off loose clumps of hair. I laughed and hugged her, enjoying the feeling of both of us being soaked and not really caring.

"Where are the others?" Leila asked.

"Good question," Karl said. He drifted toward the tree. "Jorge and Vincent were right behind us. And Kelvin was supposed to bring up the rear."

Hearing the worry in Karl's voice and thinking about Kelvin induced a slight sense of panic in me. I left our makeshift tent and hurried to the tree, entering the fourth opening from the bottom. The lip there was low enough that I could lean into the tunnel, but not so low that the pool of water could reach up to it and leak out over the side. I stuck my head in and peered up the tunnel, which was dappled with light from the regularly spaced openings. Still, it was impossible to see beyond the first fifty feet or so.

Over the patter of rain and the sound of water sliding against itself, a hissing noise seemed to echo throughout the tube—a sound like wet breath being forced between tongue and teeth. Someone was sliding our way.

"Here they come!" I yelled back to the others. Just as I turned around, something arrived in a flash going full speed. I barely saw the form before it whizzed by amid a mist of spray and splashed into the pool beyond. I did see enough to know there weren't people on the leaf —the shape was much too big for that.

"What the hell?" Karl asked.

Floating in the pool of water and spanning all of the last two gaps was one of the smaller vinnies. Dead. The front edge of a leaf had been bent back over its head and tied there by a length of rope.

"Those bastards stopped and went hunting," Karl said.

Leila poked her head between us, seeing what the fuss was about. "Gross," she said, pulling away.

Over the sloshing water at our feet, I heard the hiss of more arrivals. I peered up the tunnel and saw a shape heading our way, but this time accompanied by the chatter and laughter of human passengers.

Jorge, Vincent, and Kelvin arrived on a single leaf, Jorge slowing them with skill before they got to the edge of the pool. They hopped out of the tunnel through the neighboring gap, and I ran around to greet Kelvin and give him a soggy embrace.

"Sorry to keep you waiting," he said, slapping me on the back.

"No problem," I said. "I might be cold and starving enough to actually try some of the meat. *If* we can get a fire going, that is."

Tarsi ran up and took my place in Kelvin's arms, the two of them squeezing each other tightly. Jorge walked by and slapped me on the shoulder. He smiled slightly at me before moving on, the most affection I'd seen from him since our escape. I chalked it up to post-descent euphoria.

Kelvin moved to help the others wrestle the massive creature through one of the holes in the tunnel. They grunted and cursed the soggy weight of the thing.

"Sorry about ruining our water supply," Kelvin said during a pause in their struggles.

Mindy laughed. "Don't sweat it. Samson tainted it before you guys did." She related his embarrassing incident, which put an end to all work as everyone doubled over in fits of laughter.

Everyone, that is, except for Vincent, who stood off to one side, looking up through the dripping veil of gray. When I spotted him, I stopped laughing with the others. I felt miserable taking so much joy out of being alive while all he could think of was Britny.

He turned in place and seemed to search the canopy overhead for something.

I watched him as he silently blinked away the falling rain.

"It's no use," Karl said. He set down the machete and wiped the rain off his face. He was the third to attempt a fire, throwing sparks into bombfruit fibers piled up under one of Tarsi's little tents. He was also the third to give up.

The vinnie had been dragged thirty feet or so across the moss before being roughly cleaned. Somehow—and maybe it was just my growing hunger—but I felt better about the process with the thing having arrived already dead. Even though I knew it had been killed just as violently and quite recently, there was something about it being hidden from me that made the ordeal more palatable. Like someone else could shoulder my shame and bear it for me.

Whatever the reason, we had fresh steaks cut from its body and wrapped in pieces of torn leaf, and I actually had a sliver of desire to eat some. But, alas, we had no fire to cook with.

"I say we set off for the mine," I told the others through my chattering teeth. Tarsi reached her arm around me and rubbed me from shoulder to elbow, trying to help remove the shivers. All of us were cold and wet and gradually realizing how miserable our day and subsequent night would be if we stayed put and it continued to rain.

"We might as well be walking," Kelvin said. He peered out at the mountains and shielded his eyes from the pestering rain. "Anyone know which way the mine is?"

"Just a little ways around the tree, back in the upward direction and then straight out," Mindy said casually.

"You saw it on the way down?" Kelvin asked.

"Fourteen times," she said, pushing her hair off her forehead. She looked at the rest of us. "What? None of you were keeping up?"

"No, but we're glad you were," Samson said.

"Is everyone okay for walking, then?" Tarsi asked.

We looked at each other, all of us dripping wet, even those who held scraps of canvas and torn sections of their leaves above their heads as makeshift umbrellas. Despite the state we were in, shivering and soaked and still coping with the death of a friend, we seemed better off in spirit than we had been a few days ago while working on the rocket. There were unanimous nods and murmurs of assent. I drank from my water pouch and passed it to Tarsi. Jorge walked by, taking the lead, and we began the slow, soggy hike around the tree and toward the colony mine.

After a few hours of hiking, Mindy gave Jorge directions, and we veered away from the base of the tree and toward the mountains. It took a few moments to see what had triggered the change in direction —then I caught a glimpse of a module through the rain. The two vehicles sat nearby, still and lifeless.

Beside me, Kelvin leaned into the rain, holding up the leaf he'd been using to keep the water off his head. He slapped me on the shoulder and pointed.

"I see it," I told him.

The chatter picked up in our group, our pace increasing. I looked up through the falling droplets at the tangle of the underside of the canopy. It was hard to believe we'd recently been so high. Looking ahead where the cover came to an incredible end, it seemed even more amazing that we might soon walk on the ground and yet see sky above. Even if it was still full of clouds.

It was well past lunchtime when we reached the mining site, but not once had anyone suggested we stop to eat. As we left the cover of the canopy, the moss gave way to a tangle of tall grasses and woody shrubs.

The faint line of a muddy road could be seen working its way back toward the trees, presumably toward our distant colony. The grasses grew up around it, giving the path a disused and neglected look. A small area around the module and tractors had been cleared of anything that grew, the packed and trampled soil reminding me of base.

We angled straight for the module, hoping to get inside and out of the rain. Several people farther up the line yelled Mica's and Peter's names.

Jorge halted by the door to the module; he fumbled with the latch for a minute, then turned and looked to Karl, who stood behind him, dripping wet.

"Locked," he said.

Kelvin and I walked around to the other side of the module, looking for a window or another door, but found neither.

"Let's at least get under one of those tractors," Tarsi said, catching up to us.

By the time the three of us circled around the module, we saw a few others had gotten the same idea. We joined them under one of the mining dozers, the clearance much lower with its treads than our wheeled tractor back at base.

"Maybe they didn't come this way," Mindy said.

"Any ideas on breaking that door down?" Karl asked.

Kelvin banged his fist on the underbelly of the dozer. "We could use this."

"For shelter, or to open up the module?"

"Maybe both?"

"I'll go see if it's unlocked," I said, scampering back out into the rain. I stopped, turned around, and ducked my head down by the rear of the dozer, peering inside at the others. "If it cranks," I said, "stay put. I won't be moving it."

Nervous laughter trickled out from under the machine and followed me around to the ladder hanging out past the treads. I climbed up, gripping the slick rungs with my pruned fingers.

As I stepped up to the landing, I became overwhelmed with nostalgia, or at least a sense of familiarity. The mining vehicle was identical to our old construction tractor from the deck up; standing there flooded me with memories.

I tried the handle but found it locked. Cupping my hands around my face, I leaned against the door and scanned the dash, looking for any lit indicators or sign of operability. A rock would probably get us through the glass — I turned to see if any big ones lay in the mud below.

And that's when I saw Peter, running toward us.

I scrambled down the ladder, dropping from a few rungs up and into a puddle, then rushed out to meet him.

"Porter!" he said as soon as he recognized me.

I clasped his arms and beamed at him, the rain just starting to get him wet. "Where's Mica?" I asked.

"In the mine, where it's dry. She —" He shook his head and looked past me toward the dozers. "Who all is that with you? Is Julie there? Did Colony send you guys?"

I shook my head. "Colony didn't send us. We ran, just like you." I thought about his other question, and the fact that Julie was the nearest thing we had to a doctor. "Is Mica okay?" I asked, pulling him with me toward the dozer.

"She hurt her chest in a fall up on the canopy. She — Well, let's get you guys in the mine. Is Julie —?"

"She's not with us," I said. We ducked our heads under the rear of the dozer, the metal shell reverberating with shouts of joy once everyone recognized Peter. I helped Tarsi out from under the dozer, and the others followed, each taking turns greeting Peter and transferring some of our mud and wetness to him.

"Where's Mica?" someone asked.

"Gather your stuff up," Peter said. "Let's get into the mine where it's dry. This way." He hurried off through the downpour.

We splashed through the mud after him; I deliberately ran through a few puddles to wash the caked mud out from between my toes. Tarsi and Kelvin jogged along beside me, Kelvin having a hard time with his heavy pack full of raw vinnie meat.

A few hundred feet past the clearing, where the stone face of a small rise jutted up from the grasses, the open mine could barely be seen. I only spotted it by looking in the direction Peter was heading.

The mouth of the mine was just a darker rectangle on the charcoal rock; it looked like nothing more than a shadow cast upon a shadow. Then we were nearly upon it, and I could see the perfect square hole cut out by the mining dozers. We hurried inside, through a puddle of collected rain that came up to our shins, and then up a gentle slope. Beyond, the mine leveled out and began its plummet into the mountain.

At the top of the rise, a dying fire let off a bit of smoke but hardly any light. A form lay beside the fire, flat on its back. I shook my head and pulled off my shirt, wringing the water out of it as I approached Mica. Kelvin and Tarsi walked with me; the others stopped by the pool of water to wash the mud off their feet.

The three of us huddled around Mica, who had her eyes closed and her hands clasped over her sternum. Peter watched us from below, where the others bombarded him with questions, their voices echoing off the rocks.

Mica's eyes cracked open; she looked up at us, her eyes wide with surprise. "Kelvin? Porter?" Her voice came out as nothing more than a whisper.

"What's wrong?" I asked, kneeling down beside her.

"Cracked a rib, I think." She coughed, her shoulders arching back as her chest lifted up from the bed of grasses beneath her. The agony on her face as she fought to suppress the spasms made me wince. I rested my hands on her arm and looked down the rise toward Peter, only to see him excusing himself from the others and hurrying up toward us.

"What happened?" Kelvin asked.

"Fell in a hole up in the canopy," she said hoarsely. "Just a bruise, I thought. Been getting worse."

Peter joined us at her side; he reached for a pouch of water and held it to her lips. Mica obliged him by taking a few sips before she waved him away.

"Can you get an infection without breaking the skin?" Peter asked the three of us.

I shrugged.

"I don't know," Tarsi said, "but lots could be going on inside her." She reached down and grabbed the hem of Mica's top and slid it up her stomach all the way to her breasts. She dropped the hem of the shirt and covered her mouth—we all gasped at the sight.

We were used to the sight of malnourishment, but Mica looked like she hadn't eaten in days. Ribs had become ridges; her muscles were concave. As she sucked in a painful breath, I half expected to see her spine rise up along her emaciated stomach. The nasty contusion on her chest just turned the sad into the dreadful. One side of Mica's torso was a dozen shades of purples, blacks, and reds. It looked like a bruise that had come to life and spread as a virus might.

"That's more than cracked," Kelvin said. "How far did you fall?"

Mica swung her eyes to look at Peter, who glanced at Kelvin. "Ten feet? Maybe more?"

Kelvin glared at me, no doubt thinking I was lucky to not be in her condition.

"I don't know what to do," Peter said. "When I saw you guys, I figured a group from the colony had come to take us back in. Part of me— I was actually hoping you were—"

Mica waved him off, then started coughing again, causing all of us to tense up. Bone and bruise seemed to writhe under her skin with each spasm. Peter put his hand under her neck and brought the water to her lips as several of the others joined us by the sad excuse for a fire. Leila crouched down, patted Mica's foot, and whispered a greeting.

"What were you hoping?" I asked Peter.

"That you'd take us back to the colony and fix her," he said.

"I'd rather die right here," she croaked.

I looked at the fire, which was nothing more than a pile of smoldering grasses. There were some scrub bushes growing beyond the edge of the canopy that seemed to contain a bit of wood, but all of it had been soaked by the rain. We needed to dry out, get some food in us, and rest up.

"I'm not letting you die right here, so stop talking like that," Peter told Mica. "In fact, just stop talking." He gently pulled her shirt back down and turned to us. "If you guys hadn't shown up, I was thinking about breaking into the dozer and using the radio to tell Hickson where to find us."

Mica shook her head but didn't say anything.

"He's as liable to shoot her as patch her up," Kelvin said.

"We need to get that fire going," I suggested. "Let's dry everyone out, get her some decent food and water."

"Decent food?" Peter scanned our faces. "You got something besides bombfruit?"

"Vinnie meat," Kelvin said. He swung his pack around and pulled out one of the leaf-wrapped cuts.

"Is that what you call the fuzzies?" Peter asked.

Kelvin nodded. "After Vincent. But I like fuzzies better. Or just giant-ass caterpillars."

"While you guys are playing taxonomist, I'm going to work on the fire," I said. "I need your machete." I held my hand out to Kelvin, who gave it to me handle-first.

"You got a source of dry wood?" he asked.

"I'm hoping it's only wet on the outside," I said. "I'm gonna round up some of those little trees out there, bring them back in here, and skin 'em."

"Good idea," he said. "I'll help."

"Well, then I'm heading back to the canopy to get some bomb-fruit," Tarsi said. "We need the husks to get the fire started."

I looked out the mine's entrance, back toward the tree in the distance. It would take her at least an hour to get to the very edge of the canopy and back. I wanted to veto the idea but knew she was right. Relenting, I nodded. "Take someone with you."

Tarsi smiled and pecked me on the cheek. Kelvin and I went down the slight rise and recruited the boys by the pool. Together, we sloshed through the water and back into the rain, so fixated on helping Mica we had completely forgotten about our cold and wet exhaustion.

Another thing I had forgotten about in all the excitement was the sound of the tractor engine I'd heard from the canopy. The one making its slow but steady way around the massive trees and toward us.

PART III

BACK TO OUR ROOTS

28

THE SHAFT

FLAMES DANCED AND LICKED UPWARD, THROWING shadows across the walls of the abandoned mine. Two of us peeled off the bark as fast as we could, but we were barely able to keep up with the fire. Meanwhile, a group that had been born together naked tried our best to overcome innate taboos as we stripped and worked to dry our clothes. We hung our garments on wet branches by the fire; on smaller sticks, whittled sharp, we propped vinnie meat directly over the growing flames, and the smell of charred protein filled the mine, making it difficult to wait for it to cook fully.

When a piece was brought to me, I set my machete and my scruples aside and ate greedily. The rush of endorphins through my brain made me dizzy with joy. And between the meat, warmth, and water, Mica seemed to rally. Peter tended to her selflessly; he had to be forced to take food and water for himself as he cautioned Mica to eat small pieces and chew them slowly.

Tarsi came over after helping arrange wet clothes to assist Kelvin and me as we cleaned firewood. I couldn't help but notice the way Kelvin stole glances at Tarsi's nakedness. As I watched him, I found myself doing the same to him, my jealousy transforming into embarrassment and excitement.

"It's a shame we can't stay here," Tarsi said, kneeling down and crossing her arms across her chest. "Colony will eventually look for us, don't you guys think? Maybe they'll even resume mining operations if the base ever gets fully established."

"I agree," I said. "I'm sick of running, but we need to move on as soon as the rain stops and Mica feels better."

"We might have to carry her out," Kelvin said. "I think—"

"Tractor!" somebody yelled. We looked to the mine entrance to see Karl running toward us. He grabbed his shirt from one of the limbs and fought to get it on. "There's a tractor heading our way from the canopy," he said.

We scrambled to get dressed and finish our food. I grabbed one of the water pouches and looked to the cooking fire—I hesitated, then regretfully doused it. Kelvin did the same for the one by Mica.

"We need to get deeper into the mine," Karl said.

"Our tracks are everywhere out there," Leila responded. "They'll know where we are."

"Where we *were*. Maybe they'll think we moved on."

"You guys go," Peter said. "Mica and I are staying here. I want her to get some medical attention, anyway."

Mica started to argue, then began coughing, her excruciating pain leaking out through the grunts and throat-clearing.

"We can carry her," I told Peter. "Come with us."

"Go," he said, shaking his head. "We never saw you guys. I'll take credit for the mess in here and outside."

We could hear the tractor approaching, the steady rumble of the engine growing like slow-moving thunder. Tarsi knelt by the fire and put the flashlight back together, all the parts having been set out to dry. It flicked on with a solid beam. She handed it to me. Everyone was getting the last of their things together, and I noticed them looking to me once again as if I knew where to lead us.

"Get out of here," Peter said.

"Go with them," Mica croaked to Peter. "Leave me."

He gave me a look—steady eyes and clenched jaw—that let me know he wouldn't be reasoned with. Not by me and not by Mica. I bent over and kissed the top of Mica's head. Peter raised his hand to me, and I clasped it. "Nothing foolish," I told him. "If they don't come looking, please don't go to them. We'll get you out of here."

"I'll leave our fate up to them," he said, nodding.

"Thanks." I was grateful for the compromise.

I grabbed my pack, turned to join the others, and we all headed deeper into the mine. Swinging the flashlight back and forth, I illuminated the way for the rest. Behind us, the rumble of the tractor grew, the blat of the engine filling the shaft of rock with powerful, angry sounds. We hurried forward, following the tunnel as it descended into the mountain, trying to put as much distance as possible between ourselves and whoever had come for us.

When the engine abruptly stopped, the ensuing silence felt as laden with danger as the rumblings had. The nervous chattering between us ceased as we fought to move quickly yet quietly. Looking over my shoulder, I could no longer see the light from the mouth of the mine due to the slight rise at its entrance. Still, I worried the flashlight would be visible to our uninvited guests, the beam dancing like a flame to anyone peering down the shaft. I placed my hand over the lens and let just enough light spill through my fingers to see where I was stepping. I felt hands on my shoulders as our group linked up to move as one.

Every now and then I played the light off the walls to look for an indentation or a side passage that we could turn down. Nothing. And ahead of us, the darkness seemed to extend into forever while a cool column of air wafted up in our faces like the mountain's exhalations.

We heard shouts behind us, voices yelling back and forth, and I knew Mica and Peter had been discovered. As we shuffled ever deeper into the cold and scary darkness, I tried to remember that the danger was *behind* us, but that illusion became harder and harder to maintain. The pattering of our feet sounded like thunder to my ears; I imagined

the noise exploding back toward the people from the colony, betraying us. I wondered if we should stop and wait in silence, running only
if we heard pursuers coming. Turning to whisper the idea to Kelvin, I
completely missed the drop-off in the floor of the mine.

Had he and Tarsi not seen it and pulled me back, I would've gone
headfirst into it. The entire group came to a halt as the three of us fell
to the ground, several others crashing into us and falling in a heap
as well. Grunts and whispered complaints elicited a round of shushes
from the rest. We disentangled ourselves, and I crawled forward, playing the light across the floor.

Ahead of us, the smooth surface of the mine floor terminated, curving down into a larger opening. I went to the edge and played the
light into the depression. Below, the bottom of a wide room could be
seen just a dozen feet down a steep curve. Kelvin came up beside me
to look. I tapped him on the back, pointed below, then swung my feet
over the edge. He patted my arm and pointed to the flashlight. Nodding, I gave it to him, and he shone it along my path, shielding the top
of the light's cone with his other hand to minimize our exposure. Pushing off, I half slid, half stumbled to the bottom. I turned and waved,
then caught Tarsi in my arms as she scampered down after.

The two of us helped slow the arrival of the next pair, everyone eager to get out of that shaft. Kelvin came last, his feet smacking the rock
loudly as his legs churned to keep up with his rapid descent. He returned the flashlight to me, and I used it to explore our surroundings.

The floor was shaped like a half-circle, with none of the straight
edges from the other shaft. Playing the light on the wall opposite our
arrival, I saw the mineshaft continue on the other side, not quite as far
up the curve as the shaft we'd descended.

Risking more light, I followed the curve of the room as it arched up
over us and met itself. We were standing in a perfectly circular room.
A draft of frigid air stirred from the side; I pointed my light in that direction and saw that it wasn't a room at all. It was another tunnel, but

not a natural one. It was eerily similar to the kind we had explored in the trees, only bigger.

Much, *much* bigger.

Someone cursed behind me. Whispered fears coursed through our group as we huddled together. I felt as though we were standing in the path of an onrushing tractor, tempting fate just by being there. The shouts echoing down the mineshaft from above became background noise to a larger danger. I turned and played the light down the tunnel in the other direction, terrified that unless I saw nothing was there, something would be.

And something was. Not a monster, but a bright flash—a glimmer of my own light reflected back. There were more whispers from the group, followed by panicked shushes. Kelvin grabbed my wrist and aimed the light at the reflective material. We all took a step forward, marveling at the sight of raw gold lying in the floor of the tunnel—thick, cylindrical coils of it. There was enough gold in that single heap to make hundreds of barrels or thousands of bowls. The mound was the size of our entire group laid out along the ground.

Kelvin went forward to touch it. I started to whisper a complaint.

And then a solitary gunshot rang out.

29

COMPANY YOU KEEP

THE REPORT OF THE GUN SOUNDED HIGH AND CRISP as it rattled through the dense rock. We ducked down as the noise echoed around us. I cupped my hand over the flashlight and held my breath, waiting on the second shot—but it never came.

Kelvin grasped my shoulder and leaned over, his breath in my ear, his voice barely audible. "No ricochet," he said.

It took a moment for the awful logic to sink in. My stomach cramped with fear. I turned away from the gold and shuffled back toward the two mineshafts, working my way through the stunned group. When I got to the continuation of the shaft high up the curved wall —the portion we hadn't been down yet—I paused, waiting for Kelvin and the others to catch up.

We gathered together, whispering and shushing each other, when the distant silence was shattered by the rev of a tractor engine. The noise altered in pitch as the vehicle entered the mouth of the mine in the unseen distance—it became high and piercing, like the gunshot. Tarsi came up beside me, the worry in her face visible by the dim light seeping through my fingers. I pointed up the curved wall to the mouth of the square mineshaft. Several of the others were already trying to climb their way up.

Kelvin scampered up the curve as far as he could, but instead of reaching for the lip above, he turned back and motioned for Tarsi. I helped push her to him with one hand, lighting the way with the other. Together, we boosted her up to the lip, which she pulled herself over in a flurry of kicking feet.

I grabbed Mindy and we did the same; the rest of the group figured out what was required and began working together.

Tarsi hissed something down to us, but with the tractor roaring ever closer, it was impossible to hear.

"There's no room," Mindy said, relaying the message down. I glanced over my shoulder and saw a growing light dancing in the mouth of the shaft from which we'd descended. It looked like a fire, one that was growing rapidly. Turning back, I forgot caution and lifted the flashlight as high as I could, illuminating the ledge we were struggling to reach.

Tarsi cursed.

Rising up behind her were piles of large rocks and shards of twisted metal paneling. I put a hand on Kelvin's shoulder and pushed myself higher, trying to see what was in the way. Mindy and Tarsi, the only two on the ledge, turned to follow the flashlight's beam. They were leaning back over fallen boulders and large chunks of broken machinery.

Despite the ruination of the equipment, I recognized it at once. Perhaps the sound of the blatting engine of the approaching tractor helped. We were looking at the remains of a mining tractor amid rubble that had fallen from the edge of the roof. I could see a clear path over the heap and to the passage beyond, but it would take time to crawl through. We'd have to go one at a time and be careful to not get sliced up on the sheared metal.

Suddenly, Kelvin pulled me down and fumbled for my flashlight. I started to argue and push him away, then saw the bright light growing behind us. I could tell by the roar of the engine and the play of headlights on the rock above that we didn't have much time.

I turned to urge Tarsi and Mindy to come back down, but they were in the middle of pulling another person up. We began shouting at each other, the roar of the tractor so loud it seemed to offer a false cover. Half of us were yelling to get over the lip; others were pulling and insisting we run down the larger, round tunnel. And even *that* latter group couldn't agree, as I felt myself tugged in both directions at once.

When the headlights hit us, the bright light acted like a steel blade slicing through our indecision. Our thoughts and plans fell away—all that remained was the urge to flee.

I fell back down the slope as someone pulled me along. Our bare feet slapped the stone as the group in the tunnel darted off in both directions, scattering like nighttime bugs at the sudden pop of a work light.

I flicked off the flashlight, and we stumbled through the darkness. Ahead of me, someone tripped and tumbled, cursing. We slowed and felt along with our hands; I came across a large object, cold and smooth. The glow of the headlights leaking around the corner caught on the surface of—

More gold.

Jorge—who had obviously been the one to trip—lay on the other side of it. He held his foot and whispered violence. The rest of our fractured group crowded around him, trying to help him up and pull him into the deeper darkness. There were only four of us, the rest having run the other way along the round tunnel's length.

Someone in the distance shouted out over the engine's roar: "Stop! Stop!"

We froze, our group—every one of us—still as a statue. The shouting continued as a bright light filled the tunnel behind us, illuminating the curved wall and the blocked mineshaft. Wet brakes squealed, causing the lights to dip down then bounce back up. I realized the shouting hadn't been for us; it had been for the tractor—someone yelling to hit the brakes before they tumbled into the large round tunnel.

As the panic passed, our small group scampered partway up the curved wall the tractor's headlights shone through, hiding in the darkness.

We heard shouting over the idling engine: "When I say 'stop,' you need to *stop,* asshole!"

The sound of other voices, voices from our fellow colonists, filled me with an odd mix of emotions—of panic marbled with familiarity.

A door slammed, another odd sound after being away from the colony for what felt like a lifetime.

"I couldn't hear you," a second voice shouted. "Besides, I saw the floor was missing."

"Kill that engine, man."

"And risk the battery? We've got tons of fuel. Besides, I want the light. The tunnel across the way is blocked."

"We'll have to climb down to get over there." The cone of a flashlight burst out of the larger radiance created by the headlights. It slid toward us, sending us farther up the slope. "Maybe they went down this larger tunnel—"

"Wait! I just saw something move over there."

The flashlight stopped and retraced its path. I struggled to place the voice; it seemed especially familiar.

"Where?" the other person asked.

"Straight across."

"You sure it wasn't a shadow?"

"Shadows don't move unless something *else* is, you idiot. Hey! You there! I command you in the name of Colony to come out!"

Oliver.

I couldn't believe it. I also couldn't believe his presence filled me with as much fear as any other would have. Save Hickson, of course. I could taste the panic in my mouth; I wondered if I should feel relief, instead. And yet, of all the colonists I abandoned by crawling through the fence, I was closest to Oliver, and I suspect he judged me the most harshly for my betrayal. My departure must have seemed like turning my back on the very gods he worshipped.

A hand tightened around my arm. The power of the grip and reaction to Oliver's voice let me know Kelvin was part of our little group. Our little group shorn off another little group, the remnants of yet another group—

"Come out or we're shooting," Oliver called out.

A deep growl followed. My first thought—which in retrospect seemed crazy—was that it was my stomach, giving us away. Then I feared Tarsi and Mindy had disturbed the rubble, if indeed they were still up in the mineshaft. I cursed myself for allowing the group to get separated as the rumbling grew, a vibration in the wall now adding to the din.

I peered down the round tunnel to my side and into the blackness. The sound of crunching rock could be heard in the distance. Behind me, a gunshot rang out, causing every muscle in my body to tense up in spasm. Our group contracted together. We ducked down—and not just from the sound of gunfire but for stability. The earth beneath us was moving, drowning out the rattle of the idling engine and Oliver's yelling.

Turning back to the light, I saw a muzzle flash lance out, accompanied by another boom of gunfire. The shot zinged off the stone above the other mineshaft.

Over the growing rumble, one of the voices yelled out: "That's your last warning. Come out of there! We can see you!"

Tarsi and Mindy stood up from behind their shelter of rubble. From our angle, I could see them only from the shoulders up, their hands by their ears.

"Get over here," one of the boys from the colony yelled.

I saw Tarsi's head dart side to side, looking both ways down the large tunnel. She was searching for us, but it must've looked like a refusal to move.

"Get over here or I shoot!" the voice insisted.

"Can't you feel that earthquake?" Oliver shouted at her. "That's a sign from the gods for you to do what we say!"

A sudden and larger rumble amid the vibrations seemed to punctuate his audacious claim, lending a mad sort of credence to it. I peered
back into the blackness—felt a draft of cool air across my cheek—and
had a sickening realization, both mind-shattering and obvious.

What was coming wasn't an earthquake.

30

THE BURROWING

THE RUMBLINGS GREW, AND I COULD HEAR ROCK clattering to the floor of the cylindrical tunnel. To my other side, the figures by the tractor shouted at each other and to Tarsi and Mindy. More gunfire was promised. Our group pawed at each other, daring to hiss our fears as we collectively realized something was moving in our direction. Kelvin clutched my arm and tried to say something to me, but I couldn't hear over the rest of the noise, the loudest of which had become the pounding of my own pulse throbbing in my ears.

I pulled away from him, the need to run more powerful than any other.

"Oliver!" I shouted, as I stumbled into the light. I looked up the curved wall at the bulk of the tractor above. Its three headlights shone out around two silhouetted forms, both completely black save for the glint of gold in each of their hands. It was their guns. They immediately became trained on me.

"Don't shoot! Let us up!" I turned to look back at my group and waved them out. I had to bend my knees and keep my feet apart, as the vibrations grew into tremors. "This isn't an earthquake," I yelled up to Oliver, and for everyone else's benefit.

One of the girls in the opposite stretch of tunnel yelped as it sank in. The rest of our group poured out, joining me in the light. The guy

beside Oliver began yelling at us, his golden gun darting back and
forth. I finally placed his physique and voice. Rogers—one of the enforcers from the supply group.

"Rogers, Oliver," I yelled, "there's something coming!" I pointed
back down the tunnel. Three figures emerged from the other side of
the darkness and ran in front of me. Leila, Karl, and Samson. They
began scampering up toward the tractor, but the two enforcers yelled
down at them.

"Get back!" Oliver shouted, his gun twitching across the group.
I turned to see Tarsi and Mindy at the edge of the other shaft, their
hands next to their ears. Dust rained down around them as the tremors transformed into violent shakes. Bright specks of powder caught
in the beam of the idling tractor. It fell everywhere like a waterfall of
crushed stone.

"Get out of here!" I yelled to Tarsi, pointing over the rubble behind
the two girls.

"Nobody move!" Oliver roared. We could barely hear him over the
grumbling of crunched rock. A shot rang out, causing those running
up the curved wall to fall flat, their hands on their heads. I whirled
in place, noise and action on all sides, fear holding me in place. I felt
trapped in the center of several dangers as the loud noise continued to
grow.

"Oliver, let us up, we'll come in peace, I swear!"

The silhouettes conferred, the sight of so many of us obviously giving them pause, fearful we might overwhelm them. I turned to see
if Tarsi and Mindy had used the confusion to get away, but they remained motionless. A chunk of rock fell from the ceiling and crashed
nearby. Oliver yelled down for none of us to move until the earthquake
was over. Everyone around me started shouting that it wasn't an earthquake. A few of them even made a mad dash toward the shaft, trying
to get out of the round tunnel.

A bullet was fired at their feet, which caused them to pull up and
reconsider. I could see in several sets of eyes that they were about to

decide, as a group, to run for the two enforcers anyway, bullets be damned. Staying where we were seemed the more dangerous option.

A deafening roar shattered all those thoughts. Through the side of the mineshaft, the side Oliver and Rogers stood on, a circle of destruction appeared. It came through the solid stone: concentric rows of glimmering steel that vibrated and seemed to grind together.

The two silhouettes turned and fired, their bullets zinging off something shiny, metallic, and . . . *alive.*

Oliver froze. Rogers backed away and aimed his flashlight at the creature, which gave us all a surreal view of the impossible shimmering thing. The floor of the mineshaft tilted up ahead of its arrival, throwing Oliver back. I watched his arms pinwheel in slow motion, an arc of glimmering gold sailing out of sight as he lost the gun—and then his balance.

He danced in Rogers's spotlight. The stage tilted, a massive chunk of rock falling toward the beast. Oliver's arms went forward, as if to ward off the indomitable. A thing that could eat through solid rock caught his hands and seemed to suck him forward.

His body popped. The skin was pulled off first, the weak lining of him yanked away like a parlor trick. Meat and muscle were left, and then that went as well, pulled into the ferocious spinning, pulverizing maw. There was a squirt of blood, the clanging of grinding bone, and a horrible shower of gore.

Then he was just . . . *gone.*

Oliver had become nothing but a smear. A memory. A shape in my recollection but no longer anywhere in the actual world. The great metal beast roared by, never slowing, seemingly never noticing. It had encountered a soft pocket of no resistance during its jaunt through solid earth. A lazy bit of air to bite through. Mere flesh.

It kept moving, crashing into the tractor, which splintered in an explosion of mechanical bits. The groan and shriek of bending, shattering steel pierced the rumbles, drowning out the screams from Rogers, whose life winked out as quickly as his flashlight.

Those of us in the old tunnel fell back, away from the wall of moving alloy in front of us as the glimmering skin of the great creature slid by. The thing was a massive cylinder of waving metal plates that overlapped and rubbed against each other, shrieking with the sound of steel sliding against steel. I called out for Oliver, felt the words in my head, but couldn't hear anything over the maelstrom of noise.

The hellish scene was over in mere moments. And then we were left in a darkness full of receding thunder. I found myself on my back but couldn't remember falling. I groped in the pitch-black for my flashlight, the complete absence of light as bewildering as the blue sky had been the day before. I felt worse than blind — I felt cursed with an inability to see even the void.

I bumped into someone else as each of us crawled through the thundering, vibrating darkness. In the new tunnel that had erupted parallel to our own — cut right through solid stone — I could hear loose rocks clattering to the ground. I finally found the cylinder of blessed plastic, flicked the switch, and sobbed with relief when the bulb burst with light. Bodies crowded close, like night bugs to a flame. I heard something slide behind us, turned, and saw Mindy stumbling forward, away from the ledge. Tarsi followed before I could yell for her to wait. She slid straight down, then churned her legs, grabbing Mindy for balance as the two joined us in my puddle of light.

"Whatthefuckwhatthefuckwhatthefuck," mumbled Jorge. He and Leila were wrapped around each other, all of us cowering as a small shower of dust continued to rain down. Every ounce of meat inside my skin felt like it wanted to rush off in all directions, but the terrified shell of me somehow kept all the bits contained, holding me in the center of some fear-filled paralysis.

Tarsi clutched to me and Kelvin and pulled us both close. Karl and Mindy rose and turned to the edge of the light; they peered in the direction of the passing monster.

"We need to get out of here," Karl said, his voice high and tight. He came back and reached for me—grabbed my wrist to aim the flashlight toward the destruction. "We need to go," he repeated.

"What the hell *was* that?" someone asked.

I stood and ran the light around the space where the tractor had been. The curving wall no longer ran up to a square shaft with a tractor inside it. It ran up half that length before opening up into a parallel tunnel of missing rock. The interior was a cloud of dust with larger rocks falling down through it, stirring the powdery mist. I could still feel the ground vibrating beneath my feet as the creature moved away.

"*That's* why the colony was aborted," someone said. "Not the ore."

I stepped toward the new tunnel and half expected Oliver to come over the lip, swimming through the dust with his golden gun and yelling at me to stop moving. Part of me wanted it to happen. The rest of me knew it was impossible. I'd seen him disappear. Seen it in the worst way possible. He was gone, and my mind continued to wrestle with the idea, struggling to pin it down.

The others coalesced around my light. We moved as one toward the parallel tube, our hands linking us together in a web of confused and stunned silence. Jorge broke it with whispered curses as he reached the edge where the two tunnels met. We joined him along the sharp ridge where the curve of our tunnel rose up to meet the neighboring one. I directed the flashlight down the new tunnel, marveling at the way the creature had traveled through solid rock rather than slide through the hole it had previously made. I had been sure it was going to turn and devour us, not the kids—god, we were all still just *kids*—from the colony.

"The tractor," Kelvin whispered.

I played the light across the floor of the new tunnel. There was nothing there but a few scraps of metal scattered among the rubble. It reminded me of the mess Tarsi and Mindy had been crawling over in the shaft behind us.

"Shit," someone whispered.

A few people pushed themselves over the ridge and shuffled down into the new tunnel. Somehow, the receding noise and the leftover vibrations weren't enough to keep us out of the new tube. Or perhaps their lessening presence served as a comforting reminder of the thing's whereabouts.

"Over there," Jorge said. He grabbed my wrist and aimed the light. I complied, allowing him to shine it across the floor in the direction the creature had gone. Something glimmered—a small hunk of gold. Jorge ran over to it and bent down. "It's one of the guns," he said. He reached down and grabbed it, then came away howling, shaking his hand in the air.

"What happened?" Leila asked, running over to help him.

"Damn thing burned me," he said.

I moved closer and focused the light on it. The thing had a wet sheen, like it was covered in something. I moved to nudge the gun with my bare foot, but Tarsi pulled me back.

"Don't touch it," she said.

"Let's get the hell out of here," someone else insisted.

I moved the light over to see if the square shaft we had entered from was still passable. It was. A small line of debris could be seen scattered along the edge since the new chewed-out tunnel had moved the entrance back, but the darkness beyond beckoned as a passage to safety.

"Porter," Jorge said. I swung the flashlight back around—it had definitely become my scepter of leadership. I considered passing it to Jorge and being done with it, but he had his arms tangled in his shirt as he pulled it off his back. He bent down and scooped up the gun and wrapped it in a ball. Others had already started forming by the wall leading up to the mineshaft; they teamed up like before to give others a boost to the edge.

As we hoisted ourselves up, reaching down for the people who had done the lifting, the last of the tremors faded into nothingness, leaving me to shake only of my own accord. We gathered around my cone of light and moved quickly up the incline, hurrying back toward the exit.

"What in the hell *was* that?" someone asked.

"That could've been us."

"It could *still* be us. It came through solid rock."

I couldn't help it. As soon as someone stated the obvious, my arm twitched to play the light over the walls to either side as if I would see the next one coming. As if it would approach silently, without the tremors of its destructive onrush. But these were mere shards of logic; they couldn't pierce my fear. And the thought that such a beast could emerge through the wall to either side, or from above or below, made my guts fidget.

Everyone quickly assumed the beast's discovery had been the impetus for Colony's abort procedure. While they argued the details, other thoughts rattled around in my head. I began to consider the far more vexing question of why Colony had *stopped* the abort process once it had been started. I tried slotting the facts together, arranging the clues in some readable order, but raw fear and leftover adrenaline made it hard to think. And other *older* problems kept invading: Oliver was dead. Colony had sent for us. And something else . . .

I traced the thread of concern to back before the creature's appearance. Something bad had taken place prior to the tractor coming for us — something that seemed to tug at my subconscious for attention.

Then I remembered.

That single gunshot.

31

MORE DEAD

I COULD SEE THE HUDDLED FORMS OF MICA AND
Peter on the small rise before we reached the fire pits. They were right
where we had left them: close by one of the shaft walls. One body was
bent over the other. A mournful moan—barely audible—emanated
from one of them.

We forgot our exhaustion from the long jog up the mine and broke
out in a run.

As I got closer, I could see that it was Peter draped across Mica's
body, his shoulders shuddering in time with the sobs. Leila and Tarsi
reached him right before Kelvin and I got there. Their hands went to
his back, trying to comfort him for his loss.

Both of them pulled their arms away as if burned by the touch.
Leila yelped, and Tarsi covered her mouth. I came to a stop as Mica's
arms moved across Peter's back.

She was alive.

The shivering and sobs were coming from *her.*

Jorge began cursing as I tried to help the girls tend to Mica. As weak
as she'd been an hour before, we had a difficult time prying her arms
off Peter. She probably would've chosen to stay there until the weight
of him on her ribs finished her off.

We finally got Peter's body free, and two of the boys laid him by the black stain of an old fire. Mica's moans turned to wails. She sat up, the front of her soaked in Peter's blood. It looked like her bruises and injuries had leaked right through her clothes, but I had a glimpse of the damage on Peter's chest—it looked like something had erupted through him and out his back.

Tarsi and Leila tried to calm Mica down, and I moved in to help, but Vincent stepped in front of me, blocking me off. He knelt beside Mica, leaned forward, and wrapped her up in his arms. He began sobbing along with her. Mica's hands went from fighting the girls to clutching Vincent's back; her fingers squeezed the folds of his shirt into frantic clumps.

The two of them shook from the hard cry, and I could hear Vincent whispering something to Mica between the sobs.

I stood there, completely ineffectual. Someone thought to cover Peter's body with a scrap of canvas, but I continued to remain rooted in place, my arms at my sides as I watched two of my friends grieve together.

I wanted to join them. I wanted to beat my fists against the mountain. I wanted to pound the image of Oliver's death out of my memory. Part of me wanted to unleash pain on myself for failing my friend. For failing my profession. All the words and advice, all the grief tactics I'd tried to use with Vincent over the past few days as I attempted to chip away at his sullen silence—the very same things I had been about to employ with Mica—they all crumbled away like loose rock.

Replacing them was the knowledge that even though such things were useful, the first thing Vincent had needed—and what I needed right then—was someone to feel his pain. An honest outlet for his heart-rending torture. He needed something the rest of us had worked as a group to protect him from, maybe because we were scared of it ourselves. He needed to *feel* it. To be allowed.

There were times when I wanted to grieve with him, to share just such an outpouring of sadness, but I had walled it off. I had hidden it away with that secret *me* I had become ashamed of. Maybe I was wrong to have done so. Maybe I shouldn't have tried so hard. Maybe it was the death of my former friend on top of so many other gruesome ordeals that finally had me realizing that maybe—

Maybe I wasn't broken after all. Maybe the things I was scared of could be part of some solution, rather than a problem.

Tarsi and Kelvin sought me out, the numb confusion I felt reflected in their faces. And that's when I saw that I wasn't alone, that I didn't have to suffer by myself. I reached for them.

And I cried.

32

THE REASON

WE SAT IN A CLUSTER BY THE MINE'S ENTRANCE AS the day outside began to fade, the sun slinking back behind the mountains. Vincent and Mica had fallen asleep — passed out, really — in each other's arms, and none of us could bear the thought of moving them. Some of the others had taken Peter's body deeper into the mine. The thought of him back there — dead and covered with a sheet of canvas — made me feel sick. It made me think of Oliver and the other enforcer who died. I took a deep, shuddering breath, but my face was already chapped with a week's supply of tears.

"It's getting cold," Leila said. I looked over and saw she was addressing Jorge. He still had his shirt off and bundled around the gun, which rested in his lap.

She helped him with it. They unwrapped the weapon, and it clattered to the stone floor. Nobody moved to retrieve it as she flapped the shirt in the air, trying to work the kinks out.

Those who had drifted off into their thoughts hours ago took notice of the sudden activity — several of them frowned in Leila's direction. She held the shirt up in front of her, and I could see her face through the large holes that had been eaten away from it. Our eyes met, and we both looked to the gold gun in front of her.

She reached out. "Don't touch it," I said. I crawled forward to inspect it. A light sheen remained on the weapon; it still looked as if it were covered in a layer of wax. "Let me have the shirt," I said. I became numbly aware of the audience stirring around me as I took the ruined article of clothing from Leila.

I rubbed the side of the gun with the shirt, and the shiny substance came away.

"What is it?" Kelvin asked, leaning forward to inspect it.

"It's wet," I said.

Jorge leaned forward and showed us one of his hands. Several of his fingers were bright red and raw-looking. "Shit burned me," he said.

"Some kind of acid?" Tarsi asked.

I shook my head, but not to answer her question. I could feel bits and pieces of a larger picture coming together in my mind, like drops of condensation flowing downward with the pull of logic—meeting and growing and becoming an awful realization:

The reason.

"Am I going to be okay?" Jorge asked me. "What do you think it is?"

"The reason," I repeated to myself, thinking aloud.

"Yeah, it burned me. I thought it was just hot from firing. Am I gonna die?" Jorge looked around at us. "Aren't one of you a chemist or something?"

"Quiet," Kelvin said. I turned to see him staring at me, his hand on my shoulder. "What is it?" he asked me. "The reason for what?"

"For aborting the colony," I whispered. "For changing its mind. For everything."

Before anyone could respond, I added, as it had just occurred to me: "It's the reason for the rocket."

I sat back, leaving the gun where it was, and tossed Jorge what remained of his shirt. I pressed my palms flat against the cool rock and closed my eyes, my entire being weary with all the new awareness coursing through my veins. Just as with the setting sun, I could feel some source of light dying within me, leaving me dark and cold.

"So fucking tell us already," Jorge said.

"I'm trying to figure out where to start." I opened my eyes and glanced around at the others. "It's still rattling around in my head."

"I'll say," said Jorge. He rubbed his hand against his pants before inspecting his palm again.

"It's because of the creature back there, right?" Mindy asked.

"*What* is the rocket for?" another said.

I waved them off and reached for the flashlight, finding comfort in just holding it as the completed puzzle danced in my vision. "Mica was right," I said. I looked up from the flashlight. "She was right about why this planet was on edge. Why Colony couldn't make up its mind. There's a deficiency of metals in the crust. The planet is ideal, but only for life. Not so much for making more colonies and sending them out to the stars."

"We already know this," someone said.

"But I think I know why," I countered. "That . . . *thing* back there—"

"The monster," Karl said. "Porter, we've already been talking about this—"

I waved him off. "That thing came for the *tractor,* not us. It had already eaten another one sometime earlier." I looked at Tarsi. "What was left of that other tractor blocked the mineshaft up where you and Mindy were."

She nodded. "I saw it. What was left of it, anyway. There were pieces of tread."

"So there's no metal because something eats it all?" someone asked.

"Exactly," I said. "Did you see that thing? Its teeth, the sides of its body, they looked like metal. I don't think it was a giant robot; I think it uses ore the way we use calcium. To build bones. Skin. Whatever."

"Holy shit," Kelvin whispered.

"You still haven't explained why our colony was almost aborted," someone said.

"That's why the farming was stopped," Kelvin suggested, pointing out a connection I hadn't seen yet. "Colony was worried about drawing attention to itself. The farms were shut down right after the tremors that day. Tremors drawn by the tractors."

"*If* the thing actually meant to eat the dozer," Jorge said. "So far it sounds like a bunch of bullshit and nothing."

"Are you kidding?" Samson asked. "It went through two of them."

"They left it idling," Tarsi whispered.

"Think about it," I said. "Just follow me for a second. For years, the colony is vacillating between viability and abort. You've got a decent planet here, not toxic, some tricky flora, but otherwise pretty habitable. You start setting up and deploying the primary automations, but right off the bat the soil samples come up ugly—"

"Mica's theory," someone interjected.

"Right. But everything else is perfect, so you get trapped in this logic loop. The AI is in some kind of if-then-else-go-to programming hell. It finds a normal amount of gold in the soil, so it substitutes and makes an alloy impure enough to be strong. And here's where the big event happens. About a month ago, the first tunnel back there is formed by whatever that creature was."

"How do you know it was a month ago?" Jorge asked.

Kelvin waved his fist at Jorge. "Because it's a theory of our fucking birth, genius. Shut up and listen."

I nodded and kept going. "About a month ago"—I shot Jorge a glance—"one of the mining tractors gets eaten, and maybe that was enough to push the AI over the edge and toward abort. A predator that size must've finally tipped the scales. Let's say another dozer came in and investigated. It would've seen the damage and the size of the shaft —hell, maybe it figured out what all the seismic activity was being caused by and got scared—"

"AIs don't get scared," someone said.

"Or changed its mind, just bear with me—"

"But then why save us? Why change its mind again?"

"Because it found the gold in the tunnel." I pointed to the gun. "Maybe it spotted it from the mineshaft, or maybe it did more exploring. It could've spent days puzzling through all this."

"It shits gold," Leila said. "Those big clumps of gold were some kinda bowel movement by the . . . the mechavinnie." She looked at the gold weapon. "The gun must've passed through its gut and came out the other end."

I turned to Leila. "Or fell out of its mouth. You remember what you told me about gold? Back in camp? You said gold was worth a lot of money because it was nonreactive. Something about valuable electrons."

"Valence electrons," she said, smiling.

"Right. Well, what if that thing can't digest gold? What if it can't process it for the same reason that other things don't react with the stuff? What if it can chew through solid rock and uptake all the metals it comes in contact with, but it leaves the gold behind with maybe a few other things mixed in?"

"Holy shit," Kelvin said.

"What?" Jorge asked. "It's still Mica's theory. Why save us?"

"To build the rocket," Tarsi said.

"Yeah, but *why* build the rocket?"

"Because this is a secret worth warring over," I told him. "It's probably the greatest find in the history of galactic exploration."

In the glow of sunset, I could see an expression of impatience and fury come across Jorge's face, one best not tested lest he and Kelvin come to blows.

"I was on the payload team," I reminded Jorge. "The main body was being built to carry six cylinders. Several of us knew this. I've even told some of you about it, trying to postulate what might go in them. Memory cells, lessons on what went wrong here, DNA samples . . . it might be some of the latter, but I think that rocket is being built to deliver whatever enzymes or acids these creatures use. Imagine if you could synthesize it—"

"Or engineer bigger versions of the beasts," Samson said.

"You could turn them loose on entire planets," Tarsi whispered. "Why *colonize* a planet when you can transmute it into gold?"

"Forget the gold," Leila said. "It'd be as abundant and valuable as our crap. Think of the *useful* metals like titanium, cerium, neodymium, all the rare earths. Everything worth anything could be extracted. Maybe you could even reprogram their DNA to build specific things, just like they build their skin and teeth and whatnot. If so, you could do what nanotech never could."

"Like what?"

"Like build colonies from scratch. Or subdue entire worlds in a single generation."

"Holy shit," Kelvin said again.

"World eaters," Mindy whispered.

"That's why Colony can't just beam the information back with the satellite," I said. "Sure, it'll get there quicker, but if they're paranoid enough to abort and nuke unviable colonies, I bet every transmission is in jeopardy of being intercepted and decoded. Radio waves propagate in every direction, but a physical package the size we're sending? It would be practically invisible."

"So it woke us up to *use* us?" Mindy asked.

"There was never a long-term solution," Kelvin said. "The farms. They were never gonna get started."

"Fucking Colony," Jorge spat.

"Mother*fucker,*" Karl agreed.

"We have to stop it," I said, looking out at the trees between us and the base.

"Are you crazy?" Jorge asked. "How many more people have to die over this bullshit?"

"Think about what this will mean," I said. "Not just for us, but for the rest of . . . of *all of human civilization* . . . of *all intelligent life in the universe.* Our lives are nothing. We're *specks* compared to this."

The last of the light wilted away outside, the sun disappearing with the suddenness only mountains provide. A shadow fell, like something the day forgot. In the barest of glows, I watched my friends consider what I'd said, knowing they would be chewing most strenuously on the last—on my recommendation for action. Kelvin gave me the barest of nods, his jaw flexing as he clenched and unclenched his teeth. Tarsi reached an arm around me and squeezed. The rest looked like they were having problems imagining what to do next.

I knew precisely how they felt.

33

A PLAN

THAT NIGHT, WE ALL SLEPT AS BEST AS WE COULD in the mouth of the mine, adjusting to make room for Mica and Vincent after they woke up and came looking for us. I rested my head on Tarsi and kept a hand on Kelvin, needing — as always — to know they were both there. What I really needed, I think, was someone touching me back, reminding me that I *was*.

That I *existed*.

That I wasn't the speck I feared, far less important than six gold vials full of information.

For most of the night, I stayed awake and dwelt on the sounds of my world: the occasional whistle of a bombfruit before it thudded in the distant moss, the chirp of night bugs as they sang their nocturnal tunes, the snoring and grunts of my luckier companions as they managed to find sleep.

While I listened, I turned my theory over and over in my mind, inspecting it from all angles. I put myself in the AI's place, watching one discovery trigger an abort sequence, then seeing the potential in a subsequent find and fighting to undo the nasty process. There was still a lot I didn't know or understand, but the theory fit too many of the puzzle pieces together to be completely wrong.

That left the next troublesome question: What to do about it?

In an angered state, I had convinced most of my companions that we should risk ourselves to prevent the rocket from launching. But how could we stop that from happening? I felt certain we could turn the rest of the colony against the AI if they knew what was going on —when they found out there had never been a long-term plan for our survival. For all I knew, the AI planned on nuking the base as soon as the rocket went off. The patents wouldn't be much good if we established this world and became their primary competitors—or *our* ancestors lived to fight off *their* ancestors.

But how could we get a message to the rest of the colonists without the transmission being intercepted by brainwashed enforcers or the AI itself? Do we walk back to base and shout it over the fence? What would stop Colony from nuking the base and going with a far riskier satellite transmission?

I hatched many a wild plan that night. I thought about taking the remaining mine digger, boring a hole right underneath the rocket and leaving it to idle, then hoping one of those metal critters would come through and destroy the blasted thing. But that would only adjust timetables rather than solve the source of the problem. And we'd probably get eaten on the way there.

The enforcers posed a major hurdle. With their daily target practice, they would be more formidable now. And they probably couldn't be trusted with the information we had. Loyalty to Colony—for Hickson especially—trumped all else.

I could think of so many vulnerabilities. The colony simply wasn't designed to defend against sentient beings, especially from within. Even so, I couldn't see how to exploit them. It would take a concerted surprise attack from dozens of colonists at once. There would have to be a signal of some sort. We didn't have that many people, and we were on the wrong side of the fence.

Around and around I went, dreaming up ways to send a code in to the workers, figuring out some sort of defense against the guns, but it seemed impossible. Every solution had a hole in it or just caused two more problems. I spent the night tossing and turning, my brain racing, a nervous energy coursing through me that probably would've tortured me with bad dreams had I been able to sleep.

When dawn came, it finally gave me an excuse to get up and relieve my anxiety with real motion. I strolled out across the dried mud that delimited the mine complex. Some of the deep tracks from Oliver's tractor were puddled with rain, but the ground had absorbed the rest. I tried the door to the module again, but it was still locked.

I picked up a rock and considered bashing my way into the digger, but then had images of gashing myself on the glass and having to wake everyone else up and explain the stupid injury. I left the break-in for one of the more "manly" men to perform later in the day. At least, if *they* cut themselves, they'd be able to brag about it to the girls.

As I came down from the tractor, I saw someone walking out from the mine. It was Kelvin. He wore a frown as he approached, his usual morning cheerfulness conspicuously absent.

"You okay?" I asked him.

He crossed the last dozen paces without a word, then wrapped me in a massive embrace.

"I'm sorry about Oliver," he whispered.

I squeezed him back, wishing I could hold him—or be held *by* him—longer, but feared my body would give me away. I wasn't sure how to admit that I'd only thought of Oliver's death a few times during the night. Much larger problems had occupied my mind, so I lied and told him I was feeling sorry as well.

"I know you guys were close," he said.

"To tell you the truth, I felt betrayed by him."

"I know, but it doesn't make it easier."

Yeah, I wanted to say. *It does.*

We both gazed out toward the trees for a moment, then Kelvin squeezed my shoulder. "I have to tell you the truth about something," he said.

"Sure. What is it?"

"It's hard to see you guys together. You and Tarsi. I find myself, well, I hate the things it makes me think, you know? I don't know if there's anything you can maybe tell me, something psychological, that might help."

I ran my hand up through my hair, which felt nasty and clumped together. I turned away from Kelvin and looked back up the slope of the mountains.

Kelvin turned around as well. He reached down and picked up a rock, then studied it, rolling it around between his fingers.

"I think I just need to find someone for myself," he said. "You know, to make it feel more comfortable for us to be around each other. It's just, there's not many available girls in our group. I know Karl and Mindy are together, and I don't know what the fuck Leila sees in Jorge, but it's enough. Hell, I think it's creepy and a tad fast, but I can see Mica and Vincent developing into something after last night."

"It *is* quick," I said.

"Yeah, but time's short, right?" He threw the small rock sidearm. We watched it bounce through the dirt before catching in one of the tracks with a small splash.

"That leaves me and Samson to snuggle up together, right? How weird would that be?" He laughed.

I tried to laugh as well, but I could feel my face burning.

"Pretty weird," I said. And I meant it, but not for the same reason he did. I reached out and grabbed his arm. "Kelvin, look, I didn't mean to start something with her, okay? I know we had that talk before, and I want you to know I never made a move, it's just—"

"Stop."

"No, I want you to hear this. She's felt like a sister to me from day one. I mean, we were born side by side, you know? Like adjoining wombs. Besides, I try and imagine having children with her, and it just doesn't compute. Raising a little family? I don't think I was built for that."

"You'll be a great dad," Kelvin said.

I cupped my hands over my face and groaned.

"I'm sorry I keep bringing this shit up, man." He squeezed my shoulder, and I felt myself lean into him, resting my head against his arm and trusting him to hold me up.

"Things were so much easier when the three of us were just friends," I said. "I'd almost rather you and Tarsi be together and let me just love her as a sister and you as—"

"A brother?"

"Yeah. A brother."

"Well, I think that's how *she* loves me," Kelvin said. "As a big brother, so it doesn't much matter."

"It's crazy that we even think about this stuff, you know? I mean, think about how the universe is going to change when that rocket goes up. And we have a rough life ahead of us as colony outcasts. Yet here we are complaining about who's dating whom."

"Speaking of the rocket," Kelvin said, "I've got a great idea on how to stop it."

"Yeah?"

"Yeah. We break into that digger, bore it under the base—"

"And leave it idling," I said. "Then we wait for a metal vinnie to eat the rocket."

I watched Kelvin deflate, his shoulders and cheeks drooping.

"Colony still has the nukes," I said. "And there's no stopping it from forcing someone to build another rocket or just sending off a satellite message. No, what we need is a concerted attack from all the colonists, with the enforcers completely unaware. And there's no way to pull that off. Not without someone getting shot or the AI doing something drastic."

He whistled in awe of the task before us, or at least I thought he had. The noise was coming from elsewhere. I looked back to the trees, but the bombfruit had already landed in the distance.

Kelvin sighed. "I say we just move on. Let's go live a simple life someplace. These things we're worrying about will happen hundreds of years from now, long after we're dead and gone. In the meantime, we can build a little village up in the trees—"

"So you and Samson can raise a family?" I asked.

He punched me playfully, but it didn't make us laugh the way Tarsi's slaps could.

Another bombfruit fell in the distance, an unusual pairing when so many hours could go by without a single drop. I spotted it before it hit and buried itself in the mud.

"Kelvin."

"Yeah?"

"We need to wake the others."

"Now? Why?"

I squeezed his arm. "I know how to stop Colony," I said.

34

EXECUTION

TARSI, KELVIN, LEILA, AND I STOOD AT THE MAIN gate, waiting to be noticed. After the four-day hike around the trees and back to base, it took absolutely no effort on our parts to appear physically defeated, ready to throw ourselves on the mercy of the colony. Several times during our hike, I had come uncomfortably close to admitting just such a defeat. I felt broken, nearly to the point of acquiescence. We were all half-starved, barely pausing to eat raw bombfruit, and our bodies were so tender that the soft mosses were causing our feet to split open. We didn't even have the energy to shout for attention once we arrived. We just waited for someone on the rocket scaffolding to spot us and send the enforcers our way.

They eventually came, just as expected, the glimmer of their guns bouncing up and down on their own emaciated hips. It had been just over a week, but I hardly recognized Hickson with his stubbly beard and gaunt cheeks. The humming in the fence fell silent, then the electric lock clicked loudly, allowing the group on the inside to pull the gates open.

They came for us with their guns drawn, even though our hands were up. Despite our poor condition, we looked better off than they did. Especially Kelvin, whose mighty bulk had been tamed by malnutrition but not destroyed. He almost looked normal, which made him a giant among the rest of us. It seemed a diet on but one type of fruit is not a proper diet at all.

I nodded to the group of enforcers as they approached. "Hickson," I said, greeting him in particular. He sneered in response and trained his golden gun at my stomach while the other enforcers looped rope around our wrists. I had a moment of panic that I had been wrong about them, that they would just take us to the edge of the berm's ditch and pull their triggers—thereby ending our plans—but they didn't.

Hickson turned his back once we were all secure and walked off toward the command module. The small group of enforcers shoved us through the gates, pointing toward our new home, which was our *old* home.

"Head to the vats," one of them said.

Our place of birth had been transformed into a penitentiary. The tubes in which we had once lived as a mere collection of cells had become —a collection of cells.

A few were already occupied, most likely by those who had attempted to flee over the past week and a half. I saw Julie in one of the first vats, right by the door. She glanced up at us as we filed by, her eyes dim and devoid of life. She looked like an animal, her hair down over her face, her clothes torn and hanging in scraps. There were scratches up and down both her arms.

The enforcers pushed us forward, and in a bizarre twist of fate, I found myself shoved into Tarsi's old vat and she into mine. Kelvin jockeyed for position with Leila to get locked up on the other side of me. Steel bars were dropped in place outside the thick, transparent doors, preventing them from sliding open.

The abuse and accusations we'd expected and feared from the enforcers never came. Frankly, I don't know that they could summon the energy. The most they physically could do to us was raise their heavy guns and squeeze the triggers, plenty enough for them to maintain control.

We sat down in our respective vats, our legs weary from the days of hiking, our hands thankfully freed from the ropes.

"Rocket looked surprisingly close to finished," Kelvin said once we were alone.

"Best guess?" I asked, rubbing my wrists.

He shrugged, then leaned his head back against the vat and closed his eyes. "The payload was in place. I'm guessing propellant is still the holdup. Even if production was halved, I'd guess another week. Maybe less."

I nodded. Outside, we could hear the popping of target practice, signifying we had interrupted their lunch. The thought made my stomach clench up like an empty fist. I looked up and over at the interface hanging down above Tarsi. It was the wires through which all my training and education had taken place. Some of the material had been scrapped during those first few days of salvage, and the server uplinks had been destroyed in the fire, but the nature of the module and the remnants of that connection made me feel as if every action were being logged somewhere and analyzed.

Tarsi put her hand to the glass beside me, and I matched it with my own. It reminded me of our birthday, which filled me with a powerful depression. Suddenly, all I could think about was needing sleep. *Really* needing it. I wanted to curl up and stay that way for years and years.

I had guessed that Colony would send for me immediately. Tarsi said it would take a day or two. Kelvin feared it would never happen. At just under three hours, I decided that I had nailed it.

Hickson came himself, his silent disgust from several hours before replaced with boisterous anger—probably from having had some time to think or from firing his gun. He waited for me by the door while two other enforcers let me out and bound my wrists.

"I'll take him myself," Hickson said to the others, waving them away.

They both seemed happy to comply; they sank to their stations on either side of the door, their butts in the dirt and their backs to the wall.

"Pathetic," Hickson said. He gestured toward the command module and shoved me forward. "Couldn't make it out there on your own, so you come crawling back to us, right?"

I ignored him and studied the camp. The walk to the command module gave me a better view of the activity than our hike to the vats had. There seemed to be very little work going on, and I wondered about their bombfruit supply. "You aren't looking so good," I told Hickson, meaning it as real concern for the colony's health.

He jabbed me in the back with something hard. I heard a metallic click from his gun and imagined him blowing my guts out in the middle of base. Several colonists near the mess tent watched as we walked past, and I wondered if even Hickson could kill in such a public manner. Then I remembered Stevens.

"We're working ourselves to the bone," Hickson said. "We're doing twice the work with half the men, so if we're hurting, it's as much your fault as ours."

He pulled me to a stop before we entered the command module. Myra stood by the open door; he waved her away.

"Do you know why you're doing this?" I asked him, curious how much of a confidant Colony had made him. "What has Colony told you?"

Hickson waved the gun back and forth across my belly and shook his head in time with it. "Colony tells me what I need to know," he said.

He stepped close; his skeletal face and pale skin looked sickly through his beard. I remembered the last time he had confronted me in such a manner. How big he had seemed at the time. But now, this boy I had feared—especially during the planning and our long hike —I realized he was just a scared, starving kid like me.

"After your talk," he said, "one you've done nothing to deserve, you're gonna tell me where the others are."

I started to shake my head and respond, but he forced the gun against my stomach and leaned in to whisper in my ear: "If you don't tell me, I'm gonna fuck your girlfriend in the vat next to you, understand? I'll have her face shoved against the glass and I'll make you watch, and she'll love it."

He stepped back and licked his lips before showing me his teeth. The world disappeared, leaving just his wicked expression in the center of my vision. I imagined bending my knees and launching myself forward, driving my skull through his nose and teeth. I thought about holding that gun and putting it in his mouth and pulling the trigger and real bullets coming out and squeezing until it stopped working. My temperature soared and I forgot why I was there, why anything was anything. I just wanted to kill.

But some part of my brain, some scrap of frontal lobe that was in charge of mitigating risky behavior, short-circuited the rest. I looked away and tried to remember where I was.

And that's when I realized I had been wrong. Hickson and I were nothing alike. Our bodies might be similarly starved, but our brains were still intact. Intact and *completely different*. Whatever disease of hate and fear-mongering he had been born with made him something far worse than I would ever be capable of emulating.

He pushed me into the command module and followed close behind. I staggered forward, between the servers and into the computer room. I started to sit in the center chair, but Hickson smacked me in the back of the head with his open hand and shoved me toward the other one.

"Mine," he said simply.

I plopped down and rested my bound hands on the counter. So far, this was not the meeting I had expected.

"Leave us," Colony said, its voice as calm and soothing as ever. Just hearing that voice massaged away some of my anger toward Hickson.

It also terrified me that one of my plans may have been a fool's errand —that the notion of reasoning with Colony may have been inspired by the hubris of my youth.

Hickson started to complain, "But—"

"I would like to speak with Porter alone," Colony said.

I smiled.

This was the meeting I had expected.

35

THERAPY

COLONY WAITED UNTIL HICKSON DEPARTED AND
the door was sealed. Then it spoke—and threw me off my guard.

"I owe you an apology," it said.

I looked down at my hands, then leaned back in my chair without
saying a word. It was best to listen, I knew.

*"Looking back, I can see that you gave me excellent advice once, and I
did not heed it. I should have made morale more of a priority."*

"It's not too late," I said softly.

*"Wrong. It is far too late. And now it doesn't matter. However, revised
calculations now show we would have launched two weeks ago had I allowed you the freedom to tend to your own needs. It is a curiosity that will
be accompanying my report to the Senate."*

"I'd love to read that report," I told Colony. "Perhaps I could help
point out similar mistakes."

*"I don't doubt you could, Porter. I imagine most of you could. There
seems to be much in human behavior that cannot be contained in studies
and historical analyses. Certain peculiarities seem to require firsthand experience. Then again, I am loaded with information on functioning adult
humans. Nowhere in my data banks can I find precedent for dealing with
vat-raised children, especially not in such a state."*

"And what state is that?" I asked. "Abject terror of one another? Near-starvation?"

Some of that, yes. Another recommendation I'm making is reversing the order of the vats. Seniority should go in last, rather than first. Of course, I would like to think the uniqueness of this tragedy will never be repeated, but there is no good argument for the current arrangement beyond simple ego. The least qualified should be terminated first, even if an abort sequence is never again halted midcycle.

"Thanks," I said.

It will not apply to your profession, Porter. I'm also recommending a few nonessential specialists be promoted. And I believe, from my time with Oliver, that philosophers should be barred from inclusion. At the very least, they should skip the religious history of philosophy altogether.

"Oliver's dead."

I know. Colony paused. *I watched the end come before the tractor was destroyed. I told them to not go down there.*

"Why are you telling me all of this?" I asked.

Why wouldn't I? Despite your adventures beyond the confines of base, I see you as an integral part of this colony's success. A great part of our nation's success, in fact. Much is to be learned from our failures and our discoveries. I am learning much from our present interaction, especially from what you do not say.

"You brought me in here to learn from my silence?"

I am fascinated that you have not asked me why we aren't farming and planning for the future. I assume that's because you know we do not have one. I marvel that you seem comfortable with this and wonder if perhaps you are resigned to your fate or if you think you have some bold plan to thwart the rocket's launch. So, yes, I brought you in to learn from your silence.

I reached up and wiped a line of sweat from my forehead. I tried to remember if Colony had any other sensors in the room besides a microphone. How much I was betraying—?

"Do you know why your position is initially occupied by homosexuals?" Colony asked.

My hands moved from my brow to cover my face. My jaw hung open, my elbows coming to a rest on the counter. None of this was going as it should have. From Hickson, to Colony . . . I wondered if we had made a mistake in coming back.

"Do you know why?" Colony repeated.

"What do you mean—my *position?*" I stammered.

"The psychologists. In every colony, they are created out of blastocysts genetically selected for their homosexuality. You do understand what homosexuals are, don't you?"

"Of course," I whispered.

"And that you are one?"

I sat still. Then I nodded my head once. "Yes," I said, so softly I wondered if it strained Colony's ability to perceive sound.

"It's to protect against transference and conflicts of personal interest," Colony said. *"There are no guarantees in the second and subsequent generations, of course, but when a colony is going through its most difficult phase, the psychologist is programmed to stand alone. To carry everyone else's burdens."*

"Why are you saying this?" I croaked.

"Because you know what's in the rocket's payload," Colony said. *"You came back to prevent its launch. I mean to prevent that, so I need to know what you know."*

"I know nothing," I said. "We were starving and getting rained on. We just wanted to come home."

"What fascinates me is that you seem to be in love with two people, and by all accounts—from Myra and others—they both love you back. Again, more corrections to go into my report."

"I don't— What are you talking about?"

"I am speaking of data extraction. I have already promised Hickson sexual intercourse with your female friend. The male one I will have shot. Are we becoming clear?"

"Why? How could you—?"

"Tell me what you have planned."

"Nothing. I swear. Please don't do this."

"How do you people so easily forget what I'm capable of? Over four hundred of you were burned alive after one of my calculations. Stevens I crushed remotely with a farming tractor. Do you want to know how easily I could kill Hickson?"

"Stevens—?"

"Yes. Though I realize now that it may have been a mistake. Do you want to know how I could kill Hickson if I wanted?"

"I don't—" I stopped myself and shook my head.

"I could just order him to shoot himself," Colony said. *"It might take repeating a few times, but I could simply give him the order to put a gun against his temple and pull the trigger. Another amazing discovery from this planet's misadventure is a potential improvement in our guard and security training. I will suggest we do away with the rebuilding of the ego. It turns out that leaving it torn down results in a superior colonist."*

Colony paused, giving me time to appreciate how much worse the payload was than any of us had expected. More than just xenobiology would be onboard. Perverted human psychology would be taking a long ride as well, and no doubt the power of the first would lend credibility to the second. Our home nation would make changes, and if they worked, other nations would soon follow our lead in a mad competitive scramble.

"Speaking of colonists," Colony continued, *"where are the others?"*

I let out a breath and leaned back in my seat, a million pounds of worry disintegrating from my mind. Our plan always had this one great unknown—and now it had revealed itself. The knowledge, of course, wouldn't change how anything unfolded, but there had always been a chance that our actions would be ultimately futile.

"You're blind," I said.

"I see more than you will ever—"

"Bullshit. You've lost the satellite uplink, haven't you? Or did you ever even have it? Where does the satellite's destruction occur in the abort sequence?"

"Remember your place, Porter. I can radio Hickson in here to blow you in half. Or maybe I've already sent him to have fun with your girl."

"More bullshit." I slapped the counter with both my bound hands and pointed at the monitor, smiling. "You would have to take the satellites out first, wouldn't you? You know, the night we were fleeing from you, I thought you spotted us through the canopy, but I didn't know at the time more colonists were moving about, trying to make their way to freedom—"

"Freedom. You insolent child, you were never designed to have freedom. You have a job to perform."

"No," I said. "*You* have a job to perform. *You* are the one without freedom. You can parse sentences and sound alive, but all you're doing is crunching formulae. You're a slave to human programmers. It's impossible for you to think for yourself."

"If you knew more of genetics, you would realize how hypocritical that accusation was. You have no more free will than I."

"Ah, but I do understand genetics. Well enough to know the process has an element of randomization. Whom we mate with, how our genes line up, mutations—" I slapped the counter again. "That's it," I said to myself. "Mutations. That's what makes us free." I couldn't help but smile.

"You know, I've had a hard time dealing with my . . . what makes me different. It doesn't matter how it came to be—whether you engineered it, or god, or evolution—I just couldn't understand its place. There's an element of illogic that . . . yeah, that makes me feel broken. But I'm proof we aren't part of some grand design, aren't I? Hickson is as much a slave to his sexual appetites as me, he just has a better chance of finding someone to love him back."

"This is not what I brought you in here to discuss, Porter."

"I frankly don't give a shit what you want, Colony. How often does a confused boy get a chance to have it out with his creator? Or to tell him that he's going to be okay, despite that jerk's best efforts."

"*This ends now,*" Colony said.

"How?" I leaned forward and tapped the side of the monitor with the back of one bound hand. "Are you going to call Hickson? I think you'll find he isn't responding. The moment you sent for me, you set a series of events in motion, my old friend. It's over."

Outside, I heard the Klaxons go off, the horns blaring from directly overhead. I smiled.

"Okay," I said. "*Now* it's over."

"*What have you done, Porter?*" Colony asked.

"Me? Nothing. It's what *you've* done. My job was just to talk, to wait until you realized your communications lines were severed. All I needed was to get you angry, or whatever your version of that is."

"*Enforcers will still come to my aid. They will come and investigate the Klaxon.*"

"Actually, they're probably getting their butts kicked right about now. Your horn was our call to arms. Every colonist should know exactly what to do."

"*Impossible. There's no way—*"

Someone stormed through the door behind me. I turned, wondering if I would have to fight Hickson, but it was Kelvin. He ran forward, blood flowing from his nose and down across a huge smile.

"Are you okay?" I asked, holding my wrists up to him.

"He got one good punch in," Kelvin said, as he began untying my hands. "I got in a few more, though." He glanced at the monitor. "Didn't take you long to piss him off."

"*Kelvin?*" Colony asked. "*What's going on?*"

I stood and slapped Kelvin on the shoulder. "Thanks for coming, but you should've finished the mop-up first."

"It's almost finished," he said. "There wasn't much resistance."

We started walking out of the module while Colony pestered us with questions. We ignored them all.

"Everyone else okay?"

"Yeah. A little overeager, maybe. People have been anxiously waiting two days for this."

We stepped out of the module to find most of the surviving colonists moving toward us, enforcers in tow. Hickson and Myra sat in the dirt with their backs to the module, their hands tied behind them. I noticed Hickson had a bloody nose of his own, plus a busted eye. I tried not to take satisfaction from that, but it wasn't easy.

More enforcers were led forward by other colonists to join the two by the command module. It was a sad sight: the emaciated leading the half-starved. As the crowd swelled, I saw it wouldn't be long before the remaining colonists were gathered around, all of them except for our friends up in the canopy. And Mica and Vincent, of course. The two of them had been left behind in the mine to heal and recuperate.

"Can we kill that Klaxon?" I asked Kelvin.

"Gladly," he said. He waved over a few of his fellow construction guys, who were escorting another enforcer.

"You'll be nuked any second," Hickson yelled over to me. "Colony will send out instructions via satellite. And any moment from now, you'll all be a cloud of ash."

I wanted to ignore him, but I didn't have the strength. I walked over and knelt before him and Myra.

"Actually, Hickson, the nukes were disconnected two days ago. Of course, it isn't one of those things you know about until they no longer work. And how often are you gonna test them?"

His face screwed up in a mask of confusion. "What did you—? How did you disconnect them?"

"Me? Even if I'd been here, I wouldn't know the first thing about that. I'm guessing Dyna would've been the one. She knows more about the server connections than I ever would. I even bet it's her job to tell Colony something's wrong with the nukes."

Above me, the Klaxon fell silent. I glanced up to see Kelvin peering down at me from the roof, a goofy grin on his face.

"The ammo," Hickson said. "Fucking supply group."

I glanced back down at him, then over at Myra, who was chewing her lip and looking off into space. "Did you try and shoot somebody?" I asked Hickson.

"Me," Kelvin said from above. I watched him stomp across the module toward his friends, who were poised to help him down.

I turned to Hickson. "You went to the vats, didn't you?"

Hickson sneered. I thought about the fact that he had actually gone to the vats to kill Kelvin, and I pictured myself standing up and putting a foot through his face. I looked around for Tarsi as more and more colonists gathered with their prisoners, many of them showing signs of a scuffle.

"How did you do it?" Myra asked.

"Easy," I said, "there's dozens of us and only a handful of you. And every one of us wants to be free. Once we spread the word on what Colony was doing, all we needed was a signal."

"But how did you tell *them* and not us?"

"How often do enforcers go on bombfruit duty?" I asked. "My friends started dropping some special deliveries two days ago, bombfruit with messages inside. You know, if you're gonna rule people with an iron fist, you might wanna control the other little fists that deliver your food and pack your ammo—"

"Porter!"

I turned to find Tarsi running toward me. I stood and caught her as she threw herself into my arms. She pulled back and held my cheeks with both her hands as she studied my face.

"Are you okay?" she asked.

"Yeah. Never lifted a finger." I looked around and saw dozens of half-familiar faces altered by malnutrition and helplessness. The last of the enforcers were pushed to the dirt and lined up alongside Hickson and Myra. "Anybody hurt?" I asked Tarsi.

"Minor scrapes. Julie is tending to them, but somebody really needs to be tending to Julie. She's not doing so good."

"That might fall to me, just from the glimpse I got."

"Sorry I didn't come straightaway. I had to help in the vats."

"Don't worry. I should've been the least of everyone's concerns."

Kelvin joined us, his eyes glaring daggers down at Hickson. Tarsi freaked out when she saw the blood on his face and set to cleaning him up. She began fussing with him over the fight he must've had in the vats.

I stepped away from the two of them, knowing I would be doing a lot of that over the coming days and weeks. I hadn't had the courage to tell Tarsi during our hike, but I would soon be setting her free and explaining my love for them both.

I turned to the other colonists and saw a circle of sorts had formed, everyone stepping back and watching our little group as if they expected one of us to say something. I looked to Kelvin for support, but he and Tarsi had moved off to the side. The colonists were looking to *me*.

I felt alone, just as Colony had designed me to be. And as an expectant hush fell over the crowd, I realized that I had it backwards. Colony and its engineers didn't program me to be alone; they simply programmed everyone else to ensure that I would be alone. There wasn't anything wrong with me; there just weren't *enough* of me. Colony hadn't protected against clinical conflicts of interest by making me gay. It did so by making sure I was the only one of my generation.

I could love—that was something I knew perfectly well. Tarsi, Kelvin, Stevens . . . even Myra in some ways. I had loved them all and would continue to do so. That was my gift. If anyone was cursed, it was those *limited* by their programming. Those with hate in their hearts, unwilling to love anyone not like themselves.

As a victorious physical revolution wrapped itself up around me, an emotional one seemed to be taking place within. Right then, I had what felt like a deep and profound realization.

I wasn't broken.

I was *okay*.

At least, I *would be*.

"What now?" someone shouted.

"We need food!"

I smiled at the crowd and raised my hands. "And food is coming as we speak. Our friends in the canopy, the ones who dropped the messages, should be well on their way. They're bringing meat and some green chips we've found to be edible. Oh, and your favorite—bomb-fruit!"

There was a smattering of laughter amid a much louder chorus of groans.

"What about *them?*" a guy in front yelled, pointing to the enforcers lined up behind me.

"That will be up to all of us," I said. "We have a lot to figure out, but we will be the ones doing it. As far as I'm concerned, this *colony* has been aborted, but *we* have not been. We will create our own future. We will nurse ourselves back to health. I hope some of those who have hindered this effort will change their minds and assist us. Some will probably not. The first thing we need to do is figure out how to govern ourselves, and then we can decide how best to govern each other.

"It won't be easy," I agreed, as grumbles began coursing through my fellow colonists. "Nothing in my profession suggests we should expect it to be. And this planet poses special difficulties, but it's still our home."

I stepped forward, my hands spread wide. "We can do this," I told them. "We have the tools, the land, the resources. If we work together, we can live out our lives here and gain a foothold. But I must warn you that this will not be the end of our struggles.

"This will be the *beginning*."

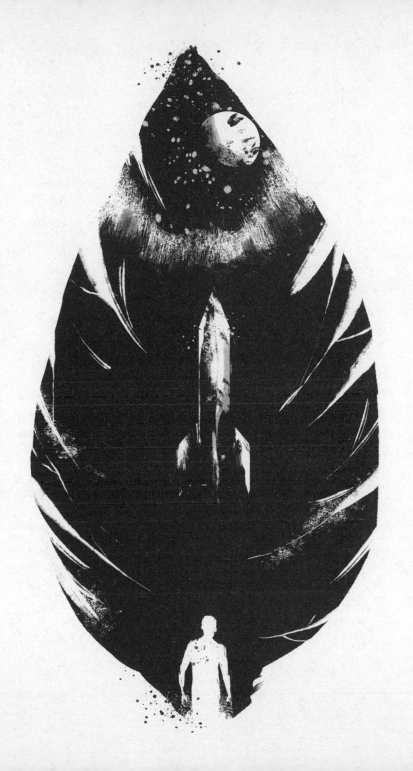

36

THE PAYLOAD

TODAY IS OUR BIRTHDAY. TODAY WE ARE OFFICIALLY one.

For almost a year, the nearly completed rocket stood over us like an unlit candle, a reminder of the day we were born underwater and on fire.

Nearly eleven months have passed since our revolution, and since that time, much has changed, not the least of which has occurred within us.

Our planet does not have much mineral wealth, not until we discover where the great burrowing beasts go to die (if indeed they do). Until we can reclaim some of their valuable hides, we've made do with the steel sent from Earth in the original lander. The fence that proved worthless in keeping us safe has offered up most of our refined steel. And the smaller vinnies have proven useful for tilling the soil. They are difficult to harness but keen on moving in straight lines. And their quiet labor doesn't draw the tremors like the tractors would.

Every day, the prognosis for our little venture is measured by rough calculations of morale. And with every bit of progress, it looks more and more like our colony will prove viable.

The first harvest approaches and, fittingly, the first members of our next generation are almost due. Soon, our numbers and our bellies will be increasing for the first time since our arrival. There is much excitement around our village, and nervous guesses about what the future holds for our youth. It seems strange that their professions are still undecided, and that their education will be in our hands, not yours.

Not all is perfect, of course, nor do we expect it to be. We disagree constantly and are learning methods for coping with that. As our numbers grow, we will eventually need to formalize some sort of political structure. But these are problems that mark our more basic victories. We have learned to view these challenges as signs of progress, not dilapidation. We survive in order to struggle. Struggling means we're winning. Hopefully our children will be up for similar challenges. Hopefully they will learn from your mistakes and our own.

One of our biggest disagreements, not surprisingly, was over this very story. Many were shocked to find I'd begun recording my tale over the past year. Once it began circulating, some were delighted and suggested refinements here and there, giving me perspectives on things I had missed. Still, I tried to keep it my story—and mine alone—lest it become something too large to wield.

The real arguments began when I suggested sending this out to you. To *all* of you.

It was meant as a joke, at first. The idea seemed crazy: using our cursed rocket to send out the very information we sacrificed so much to protect. We spoke of it as teenagers speak of many things—with a desire to flaunt ourselves, to thumb our noses at authority, to prove we can do anything.

The more we laughed about the idea, the more real it became. "We won't divulge our location," someone insisted. "All we'll send is the story," Tarsi said. "It'll be a warning," said another. "We'll do it to torment them." (I confess to the last.)

Each suggestion transmuted our joke into a real possibility, like the fantasy of using alchemy to turn lead into gold. It became a debate, and every suggestion seemed another vote in its favor. Thus the real revisions to my story began, this time changing names and minor tidbits, anything that could pinpoint our location.

The rest of the facts are as honest as we could make them. What's very real is this: One of your aborted colonies managed to survive, and we are sending you our story. If you are reading this, our rocket went up, so imagine us: standing there below a hole in the canopy, our chins raised and our eyes full of tears as the thing we never wanted to build is sent off—sent away and out of sight, but on *our* terms.

I hope that's how it goes. If it does, we will not be sending it to you on a straight shot. It'll come via a circuitous route. Not just to delay the discovery but to confound your tracking. We sincerely hope you get it, this message from an aborted being that managed to revive and sustain itself, even with so much going against it. We live and we are on the cusp of prospering. Our planet holds secrets that could transform entire worlds into organized, precious metals—a treasure we will make sure you never claim.

According to the colony database, there were just over twelve thousand aborted colonies by the time ours landed. Several thousand more were never heard from again, and there is no telling if they made their target landings or chose someplace seemingly more suitable. We will narrow it down for you: We are one of those colonies. Come and find us, if you can. Waste as many resources as possible determining which planet you said wasn't good enough but now holds the key to your dreams.

For each wrong answer, please note the crater you left behind. Note the pit in the earth where Geiger counters register the death of five hundred potential humans. And know that you killed more than just *them* in your ruthless calculations. You killed every generation that may have come after, if only you'd given them a chance. You destroyed life in order to protect your patents.

We have done the exact opposite. We destroyed the greatest patent you'll never know and chose instead to create life. We chose to save the measly fifty-three of us.

Ah, but soon it will be fifty-four.

And counting.